SHURI

SHURI

THE VANISHED

BY NIC STONE

SCHOLASTIC INC.

FOR MY BELOVED CHARLOTTE MACKENZIE.
AKA: QUEEN CHUCK. COCO LOVES YOU.
—NIC

All rights reserved. Published by Scholastic Inc., *Publishers since 1920*.
SCHOLASTIC and associated logos are trademarks and/or registered
trademarks of Scholastic Inc.

ISBN 978-1-338-85609-5

10 9 8 7 6 5 4 3 2   24 25 26

Printed in the U.S.A.   40

This edition first printing 2022

Book design by Katie Fitch

THE HIVE
ASTRO
OPTICAL
NONOPTICAL
ASTROPHYSICS
PHYSICS
CLASSICAL
MODERN
ORGANIC
INORGANIC
OFFICE
SPA
TECHNOLOGY
MATHEMATICS
METEOROLOGY
ECOLOGY
GEOLOGY
HUMAN EPIDEMIOLOGY
ENGINEERING
ROBOTICS
V.R.
HYDROGEN HALL
ZOOLOGY/ BOTANY
OCEANOGRAPHY
ELEVATOR
ATRIUM
CHEMISTRY
BIOLOGY
EARTH SCIENCE

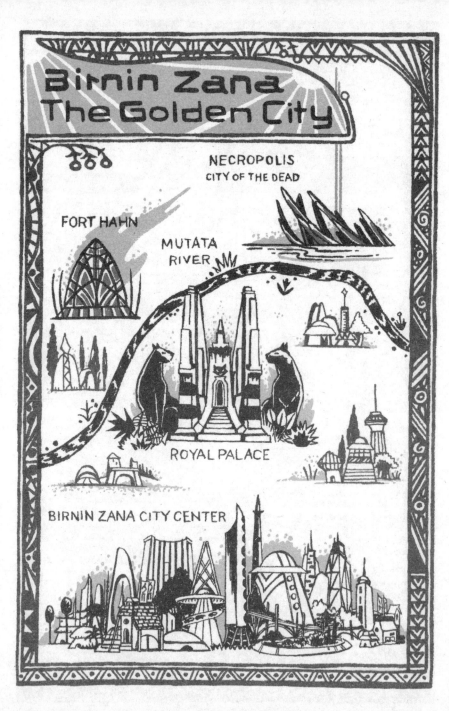

PROLOGUE

There is something seriously wrong with Shuri's best friend.

The princess and the Dora-Milaje-in-training have sparred before, sure . . .

But never like this.

As Shuri's eyes trace over K'Marah's stone-set face, her pulse quickens. Gone is the usual twinkle of mischief in the macadamia-shell brown of K'Marah's irises. Gone the dimple that appears with her slight smirk . . .

Gone even the vaguest hint that K'Marah *sees* Shuri standing before her.

It's like looking into the gaze of a complete stranger.

The girl who has stayed doggedly loyal to the princess for over three years is not the girl standing before her now. And Shuri knows it.

Knows it like she knows that the absence of her *friend* is Shuri's own fault.

The bell chimes.

Perhaps if Shuri had just listened, had shown some "concern," as her friend put it, K'Marah wouldn't be launching herself forward as though she's ready to tear the princess limb from limb.

Shuri isn't ready.

K'Marah strikes hard and fast with a chop to the tender space between neck and shoulder. And as if that wasn't enough to knock Shuri to her knees, the subsequent knee to the midsection certainly is.

Shuri stares up at the ceiling, too stunned to move.

"Fight *back*, Princess!" K'Marah's face appears above Shuri's, but the voice coming out her mouth isn't her own.

"Yeah. If you won't fight for *us*, at least fight for yourself . . ." Another voice Shuri doesn't recognize from a girl who has just, *poof*, appeared beside K'Marah.

"You're so big and bad, but you won't even look for us." A third girl.

Shuri shuts her eyes in the hope that when she opens

them, the additional girls will have disappeared. (Because who *are* they and where did they even come from?)

"Oh, is she sleeping now?" comes a *new* voice. (Shuri shudders.) "Typical."

Shuri peeks out of one eye. There are now eight girls above her—of varying heights, complexions, and ethnic backgrounds—and as she watches, more appear.

They're all beginning to shout now. And draw closer. Soon they'll crush her beneath them.

Which is when Shuri locks eyes with K'Marah . . .

Who stands tall, draws her foot back as far as it will go, and then swings it forward into Shuri's ribs.

MISSION LOG

THIS IS ACTUALLY FAR MORE DIFFICULT THAN I ANTICIPATED.

Everything hurts. I spend hours per day getting my butt kicked from multiple directions. And the minutiae of courses like Wakandan Diaspora and the World (because apparently there *are* people who have left this place over the millennia) are so boring at times, it feels as though my brain will ooze out of my ears.

I knocked an elbow out of socket in acrobatics last week—glory to Bast for our speed-healing technologies, because, *OUCH*. I also took a kick to the thigh that left a bruise the size of a mango (thanks, K'Marah!). And to top it all off, when I began to doze in Scholar M'Walimu's Governing Fundamentals tutoring session, the old man made me "sit" against the wall with no chair until my legs felt like I'd dipped them in lava, and I cried out in agony. Mean as a poked rattlesnake, that one.

But it will all be worthwhile. When trouble comes a-knocking in our great nation, I will be well prepared to answer the door (with a double backflip and roundhouse kick to the throat while spouting off the origins and attributes of our tribes, no less).

And a-knocking it shall come. Especially if the intel I just received from my latest invention is any indication. It is a multi-point surveillance system I call P.R.O.W.L.: *Panther Reconnaisance Operative Watch Lattice*. Thanks to the ant-size "bugs" I may have planted during my visit to the throne for a training-progress meeting with T'Challa a few days ago, I just overheard a conversation he and Mother were having about some top-secret international summit he plans to attend.

The conclave, he said it's called. *A gathering of hundreds of global heads of state.*

Which would likely be the most boring thing on all of Earth if not for two reasons: (1) The main topic of discussion? Technology and its implications on national security—aka my area of expertise. And if that was not enough to pique my interest (it was): (2) T'Challa told Mother he intends to seek counsel from a few of the leaders he "trusts" about the wisest approach to revealing our existence to the rest of the world.

This latter piece did come as a bit of a surprise to *me* (though perhaps it shouldn't've—T'Challa has never been one to *not* carry out a plan of his own devising). It hasn't even been half a year since we were invaded and almost overrun by a handful of neighboring nations who *do* know we are here. I was tempted to give him a Kimoyo call and ask if he's forgotten that our beloved sacred field has only grown to 75 percent of its former glory (and all thanks to *me* . . . and K'Marah . . . and

"Ororo Storm," as K'Marah calls the queen of Kenya, but my point is clear).

I'd *thought* that entire ordeal would cause big bro to reconsider his plan to expose us to *more* (potentially) hostile entities with, like . . . armies and guns and warped ideas. I recently completed a study module about the history of colonization on the continent of Africa, and it was enough to give me nightmares. Ghostly pale, blank-eyed zombie creatures clawing and blasting their way through our land in pursuit of Vibranium while asserting that *our* culture and traditions are inferior to their people-eating ways.

Just the thought makes me want to move our entire civilization underground.

But T'Challa will do what T'Challa will do. I am trying to "maintain an open mind," as K'Marah says, and consider that his motivations are beyond my informational reach . . . But this *is* the same guy who shirked my concerns when the heart-shaped herb was being decimated by a mutated toxin.

If our king is bent on exposing Wakanda

to the ugliness and greed that permeate the wider world, the least *I* can do is make sure there are minimal holes in our cyber and border defenses. Which is why it is imperative that I attend this conclave. As I mentioned before: Tech—especially the national security-related type—is *my* realm of mastery. Case in point: Large-scale tests of my security dome prototype are set to begin in a few weeks' time.

I *must* be at T'Challa's side during this conclave. It is my duty.

Otherwise this overfilled brain and aching body are in vain.

1
STIPULATION

As it turns out, eavesdropping on highly confidential conversations can cause quite the distracted mind. Which Shuri is learning the hard way: The princess's lack of focus just landed her flat on her back. Hard enough to knock the air from her lungs.

"What is going *on* with you?" Shuri's best friend's brown face appears above hers—you know, after the swirling stars have cleared from her vision and she can actually see again. "You are maddeningly distracted today, Shuri," K'Marah says. "At least block a blow every now and then? Kicking your butt over and over is exhausting!" K'Marah reaches a hand down to pull Shuri to her feet.

"Sorry," the princess mumbles.

"You certainly are!" Kocha M'Shindi rumbles. And despite the fact that the little woman only comes up to Shuri's chin and has to be close to ninety years old, the princess shrinks into herself. M'Shindi has been training Black Panthers for as long as . . . well, no one really knows, but Shuri's brother, father, and grandfather were among her pupils. One wouldn't think it looking at her aged face and tiny frame, but her area of expertise is hand-to-hand combat.

What Shuri *does* know is that getting to train with THE Kocha is a huge privilege. One she's currently squandering.

"Welp, you're in trouble now," K'Marah whispers as M'Shindi approaches with the graceful precision of a tightrope walker. Both girls have snapped to attention: backs straight, chins lifted, feet shoulder-width apart, and hands clasped behind their backs.

Not really breathing.

M'Shindi's eyes narrow as she steps right up to Shuri. So close, it makes goose pimples erupt all over the princess's arms. "Look at me, child," the woman says.

Almost against her will, Shuri's eyes drop and lock onto the Kocha's. They're so dark, it looks as if there's no barrier between iris and pupil. And with M'Shindi standing there, just *staring* at her, Shuri finds herself wondering just how much those eyes have seen.

What they're seeing right now.

"You are burdened, Princess," the woman says.

"Uhhhh—"

"Do not speak. Listen only."

K'Marah coughs beside Shuri, and the princess wishes she could get her elbow to shoot out in a quick jab to her best friend's ribs, but she's frozen under the Kocha's gaze.

"You have many gifts. Do not permit their investment in unworthy pursuits."

At this, Shuri's eyes drop, and the insectlike devices she created to give her access she's maybe not supposed to have crawl to the top of her mind unbidden.

Except her bugs are *necessary*. Without them, she'd have no idea what's really going on. *Despite* the fact that Shuri recently saved the nation—literally—Mother and T'Challa are still reluctant to share pertinent intel with the princess. Besides: It's not like Shuri intends to do anything bad with what she overhears. If anything, she's trying to make sure the "gifts" Kocha M'Shindi mentioned are actually being utilized for the *good* of Wakanda. For its *protection*.

Isn't she?

"Take heed, Panther Cub," the Kocha continues. "Unworthy uses of your gifts won't merely distract: They will serve to keep you small in your own sight. Understood?"

Shuri nods despite the fact that she has no clue what the old woman is talking about.

"Use your words," M'Shindi admonishes.

Shuri clears her throat and forces the words to form on her tongue. "Understood, Kocha."

"Lift your eyes and try again."

After a *very* deep breath, Shuri does as she's told. Looking right into M'Shindi's black pools, she says again: "I understand, Kocha M'Shindi."

The lines in the woman's face deepen as she grins, and it's then that the princess knows she has failed a test she had no idea she was taking. "You do not," the Kocha says with certainty so absolute, her chin rises in triumph. "But you shall."

And she turns on her leather slippers and silently pads away.

The whole exchange—and K'Marah's cheeky "Dang, Princess, you got *told* . . ." response—puts Shuri in a sour mood. Which just strengthens her resolve to convince Mother and T'Challa that she should be permitted to attend this conclave thing.

In fact, as first in line to the throne, it's vital that Shuri be privy to matters of diplomacy. And honestly, it's not as though she's surprised Mother and T'Challa didn't think to make sure she's included. Among the other things she's overheard through the use of her bugs are discussions about whether allowing her to train was the right thing to do. Despite the "promise" she's shown (T'Challa's word) and the fact that her dear brother is insistent on tossing himself into the line of fire (Shuri's assessment, but a valid one), Mother still isn't convinced this is the proper path for her only daughter.

So Shuri will have to prove (again) that she's ready for a higher level of responsibility when it comes to matters of domestic importance. Especially the tech-related ones.

Besides, if there's one area where her "gifts" have proven useful, it's in the area of national defense. If there's one thing Shuri has learned from her various history courses, it's that people can be downright predatory when there are valuable resources to be had (and while Vibranium has no "market value," as they say, she's *sure* it's monetarily valuable considering even the limited things *she's* been able to do with it). Full fortification will be of utmost importance.

So committed to her mission is the princess, she

takes the time to write out and rehearse exactly what she'll say. Then she showers and puts on one of the unnecessarily ornate getups that appear in her closet every few weeks: a blue-green satin beaded tunic and slim-fit trousers with reinforced knees.

She even fixes her hair.

Ayo's eyebrows rise when Shuri steps out of her chambers.

(Another thing that hasn't changed: the presence of a Dora Milaje guard within thirty meters of the princess at all times.)

And as the young royal and her beautiful, bald bodyguard fall into step side by side, the Dora speaks. "Forgive my impropriety, Princess, but did I miss a memo?"

"Huh?" Shuri replies.

"You seem . . . overdressed for a mere weekly progress-reporting." Shuri catches the woman's smirk out of the corner of her eye.

"Oh. I, umm . . . Well . . ."

"No need to explain yourself to *me*. You look very nice, is all. Teal is definitely your color. Makes that melanin really *pop*."

"Oy, you sound like K'Marah."

Ayo laughs. "I will admit: Your young friend is rubbing off on all of us."

Which makes Shuri feel a bit . . . funny. Not that she doesn't love and admire her best friend, but it hasn't escaped Shuri's notice how many other people—adults especially—have come to admire K'Marah as well. Especially since the whole Princess-and-Dora-Milaje-in-Training-Save-Entire-Nation thing. It's like K'Marah is hailed as some conquering heroine returned home from a most treacherous battle, but Shuri is still . . . just some kid.

She attempts to swallow the bitter taste in her mouth as she and Ayo round the final corner and approach the throne room door.

Which is standing open. Shuri can see T'Challa all kicked back on his fancy throne like the king he is, with the queen mother daintily perched at the edge of her lavish purple-velvet-upholstered seat. Ramonda looks Shuri over from head to toe and smiles as her daughter crosses the threshold, and then gestures to the chair on the other side of T'Challa.

By the time the princess is seated, the massive double doors have been pulled shut. The three royals are alone now.

Shuri opens her mouth to speak . . . but doesn't get the chance to.

"So," the queen mother begins, clasping her hands in her lap. "I spoke with Kocha M'Shindi this afternoon."

And just like that, the entire spiel Shuri spent hours rehearsing has—*poof*—vanished from her mind. There is only panic now. "What . . . did she say?"

Shuri's whole plan is over. Ended before it could begin. There's no way she'll be able to convince her mother and T'Challa to allow her attendance at the conclave if the Kocha told her mother she'd spent today's training session getting pinned over and over again by a girl four inches shorter than she is.

Again, K'Marah is the mighty warrior, and Shuri is the bested (and distracted) weaker foe. She sighs as her vision blurs, then makes to wipe something out of her eye before any tears can fall.

"She says that she is deeply impressed with your progress," the queen mother continues.

"Great," Shuri grumbles. But then her chin lifts. "Wait. Come again?"

Now Ramonda is smiling. "She said that you are—and I quote—'the quickest study' she's ever encountered."

T'Challa *hmph*s. He trained under M'Shindi, too, after all.

"I am very proud of you, Shuri," the queen goes on. "As you know, I've had my qualms about you subjecting your body to physical violence and adding all those additional subjects to your course load. But perhaps I've been shortsighted."

"I'd like to go to the conclave," Shuri blurts.

The queen mother draws back as though the declaration hit her like a punch. She and T'Challa exchange a glance Shuri can't read; then the king turns to his sister. "Conclave?" he says.

So that's how they want to play it, eh?

"You are going to an international conclave on tech in two weeks' time, yes? I would like to accompany you."

"Hmmm." T'Challa leans forward, placing his plum-colored-silk-clad elbows on his knees. The queen mother has gone stock-still. Not a good sign. "Now let's say, hypothetically speaking, that I *am* going to an 'international conclave,' as you put it. Where exactly would you have acquired this knowledge?"

Oh boy. In her rush to devise a scheme for getting *to* the conclave, Shuri hadn't considered that she'd need a viable (cover) source for the information. Seems quite obvious now but . . .

"K'Marah told me," she says.

"Did she, now?" The queen turns to T'Challa.

And now Shuri has to backtrack: Getting K'Marah into trouble certainly isn't what she was going for. "Not that she *wanted* to tell me," Shuri goes on, spinning a larger web. "I could tell she was excited about something, so I poked and prodded until she told me. Don't be mad at her, though. I can be very persuasive."

The queen mother's eyes narrow, and her lips part—surely to shut the princess down with gale-winds-level force.

But T'Challa speaks first: "Fine."

Mmmm . . . "Fine?" Shuri replies.

"You may accompany me with one stipulation."

Now the queen mother looks shocked. But she doesn't interject.

"Okay," Shuri says, her excitement beginning to build. "What is it?"

"You must complete Phase One of your training and earn all 'exceptional' marks on assessments before we depart."

2

RED ALERT

Fourteen days.

That's how much time Shuri has to complete three combat modules and ace four fairly intensive courses: Wakandan Diaspora and the World; Diplomacy 101: Historical Causes and Prevention of Warfare; Vibranium: Origins, Potentiality, and Limitations; and Gods and Ancestors: A Guide to the Orisha and Djalia. The Vibranium assessment is one Shuri could ace while unconscious and wandering around the ancestral plane, but the others will require some deliberate study. Especially the diaspora one.

The princess has no problem learning things that require problem solving of some sort, but just remembering things and regurgitating them? On her last assessment, she attributed the first Wakandan expedition to the North Pole to a guy who attempted a coup in the seventeenth century. (Whoops!)

As she leaves the throne room, more resolute than ever, Shuri plans the rest of her day. She can *do* this.

"So the outfit worked," Ayo says with a smirk.

"Oh, shh," Shuri's replies. But she's totally smiling, too.

"Is there anywhere you need to go before we return to your chambers?" Ayo continues. "According to my schedule . . ." She taps a Kimoyo bead on her bracelet, and a glowing list appears above her wrist.

Shuri sighs. Oh, to have her freedom back.

"Yes, okay," Ayo goes on. "Looks like you have ninety minutes of downtime . . . well, technically eighty-seven now. Then your Diplomacy lesson with Scholar M'Walimu—"

"Blegh."

Ayo laughs. "Trust me when I say I understand, Princess. I'm almost certain the old man struck terror in the dinosaurs. He has definitely been around long enough."

Shuri smiles. As far as glorified babysitters go, Ayo's not so bad.

The Dora returns her attention to the floating agenda. "After Diplomacy, you have supper, and then a private Yoga and Strike Precision session with Okoye. Anything you need to do now?"

Despite her slight annoyance, Shuri is secretly glad to hear the rest of her day read aloud. It's helping her to strategize. "I'm going to go study," she says. Of the eighty-two minutes she'll have by the time she reaches the mini-lab in her closet, she can spend seventy-five with her head in a book or two.

K'Marah would be appalled.

"As you wish," Ayo says, leading the way back to the princess's chambers.

As they walk the final hallway, Shuri's mind whirs until Kocha M'Shindi's lined face has made its way back to the forefront. After all that talk of *burdens* and *unworthy pursuits* and Shuri's lack of *understanding*, she gave Mother a good report? Why would she do that?

And more disturbing to the princess's more rational inclinations: What exactly did the old woman see when she looked into Shuri's eyes?

To her own shock, Shuri finds herself standing in front of a full-length mirror she typically avoids.

One thing is for sure: Ayo was right. Teal is definitely Shuri's color.

"Huh," she says to her reflection.

She's also gotten stronger. She stands taller, and her arms look a bit less string-beany. It's strange: *seeing* the transformation from her training taking place. She still has no idea what Kocha M'Shindi was referring to with her frustratingly obscure jibber-jabber about Shuri's *gifts*, but in this moment the princess feels as though she's seeing herself clearly. In her fancy outfit with her chin lifted, it's clear: Shuri is a Wakandan royal.

She *can* nail her assessments in the allotted time.

Without changing her clothes—which is what the *old* Shuri would've done the moment her chamber door was closed—Shuri goes into her closet to retrieve her Gods and Ancestors textbook from her knapsack.

Which is when she notices the red dot blinking on the screen of her Kimoyo card.

She freezes. More out of surprise than anything. The card is connected to a different part of her P.R.O.W.L. system: one she has set to monitor activity in every nation where Wakanda has known enemies *and* allies. The network is connected to every major news outlet—and in the cases where she was able to secure access, a few governmental entities—with alerts set to ping whenever certain keywords are mentioned: *Wakanda, T'Challa, Shuri, Ramonda, Hatut Zeraze, White Wolf, Dora Milaje, Queen Ororo, Zanda, Narobia, Vibranium,* and a handful of others.

This is the first time she's received an alert since setting the thing up two weeks ago. In fact, until now, she'd wondered if it was even working.

She takes a deep breath before approaching the work desk, now utterly terrified of what she's about to discover. What if it's some multinational plot to overtake Wakanda, imprison everyone, and sell off all their Vibranium to people who still have antiquated ideas about how "uncivilized" people on the continent of Africa are? The princess has been learning all about nuclear weapons. With what she knows about the sound-absorbing nature of the celestial substance she uses in so many of her inventions, she's fully aware of how awful it would be for the resource to wind up in the wrong hands.

"Okay," she says, wiping her damp (and trembling) palms off on her trousers. "Better to know than not know, right? Worst-case scenario, you run straight to Mother and T'Challa and tell them what you've learned."

She nods and reaches for the device. Shuts her eyes as her hand wraps around it, and doesn't open them again until she has the thing held up to her face.

Of course, she's holding it backward.

She huffs and flips it around. Then exhales. The alert is from Kenya.

An ally.

Though when the princess reads it, her eyebrows pull together.

The word that pinged was *Ororo*, but the alert . . . isn't about the gorgeous mutant woman who has power over the weather.

ALERT: KEYWORD *ORORO*
LOCATION: HAIPO, KENYA; METEOROLOGICAL
RESEARCH CENTER
TIME: 09:19
TRANSCRIPTION:

"...*ORORO* SHOULD HEAR OF THIS. I MEAN NO DISRESPECT TO OUR QUEEN, BUT SHE GAVE [UNABLE TO TRANSCRIBE] YOUNG LADY TO BE PLACED IN SUCH AN ELEVATED ROLE. I WAS OF THE OPINION THAT THE GIRL [UNABLE TO TRANSCRIBE] MATURITY—"

"WE ARE WELL AWARE OF YOUR OPINION. YOU VOICE IT [UNABLE TO TRANSCRIBE]."

"WELL, IT WOULD SEEM MY INSTINCTS WERE CORRECT. [UNABLE TO TRANSCRIBE] DAY FOUR THAT SHE HAS BEEN A—WHAT'S THAT

PHRASE USED IN AMERICA? *NO CALL, NO SHOW?*"

"PERHAPS SHE IS ILL—"

"WELL, SHE COULD SHOW A BIT OF DECENCY AND AT LEAST [UNABLE TO TRANSCRIBE] PHONE, COULD SHE NOT? SHE IS OUR CHIEF RESEARCHER!"

"I WILL LOOK INTO HER ABSENCE. THERE IS NO PURPOSE IN TATTLING TO QUEEN *ORORO* [UNABLE TO TRANSCRIBE] MORE PRESSING MATTERS."

"THIS WEEK WILL GO ON RECORD AS THE HOTTEST [UNABLE TO TRANSCRIBE] NATION! AND YASHU—"

"YASHA IS HER NAME."

"YASHU, YASHA. [UNABLE TO TRANSCRIBE] FACT REMAINS: SHE HOLDS A POSITION OF UTMOST PRESTIGE AND RESPONSIBILITY! FAILURE [UNABLE TO TRANSCRIBE] UNACCEPTABLE—"

END TRANSCRIPTION.

For a beat, Shuri stares, baffled. Then she rereads. Yasha.

If this is the same grumpy girl Shuri and K'Marah shared a meal with while visiting with Ororo in Kenya during their quest to save the heart-shaped herb, her missing four days of work does seem . . . out of character. Though Shuri hates to admit it, she *did* see a bit of herself in the older girl when they met, and there's no way the princess would voluntarily spend four days away from her lab and research.

Another thing Shuri hates to admit? She's concerned.

Which doesn't make *sense*: For one, the princess has zero relational ties to the older girl. In fact, Shuri has a hunch even Yasha would roll her eyes at the thought of the Wakandan royal being "concerned."

Besides, there are significant unknown variables at play. Perhaps she *is* sick. Or maybe she got tired of being demeaned by whoever was going on about Yasha's not being the right person for her position (surely some cranky, old-fashioned *man*). Shuri knows from experience that those kinds of attitudes definitely leak into the way people treat one another. *She* certainly wouldn't want to work in an environment where some grown-up full of opinions was constantly looking down their nose and questioning her *maturity*.

Shuri dismisses the alert. Whatever the cause of Yasha's absences, the Wakandan princess is *sure* it's nothing serious. And anyway, even if it *is* serious, it's not as though there's anything the princess can do about it from Wakanda. She and K'Marah might've managed to sneak out of the country before, but with a Dora Milaje always nearby now, the same feat is virtually impossible.

She places the Kimoyo card facedown and shakes her head. Attempts to refocus. After her training time with Okoye this evening, she will add additional keywords and tighten the parameters of the P.R.O.W.L. system so that it won't ping over something as mundane as a teenage girl not showing up for work.

Then she grabs the book she came in for and heads to her window seat to spend the remaining seventy-one minutes of her break imagining the Djalia—that elusive plane of Wakandan memory where the spirits of the ancestors are said to reside—and memorizing the attributes of Wakanda's gods.

3

COINCIDENCE

The rest of Shuri's tightly scheduled evening goes off without a hitch (though she might've hyper-extended a hip during her kick precision drills).

But her night gets overrun by strange dreams.

All involving Yasha, chief researcher of meteorological phenomena in Haipo, Kenya.

It surprises Shuri that she has a clear memory of the older girl's face, but there it is, tinted a putrid green, covered in boils, and full of rage.

Yasha is also as tall as Wakanda's seven-story capitol building.

Shuri has no idea where they are or what time of day it is, but there's a storm swirling overhead, casting the surroundings in shades of gray. She watches on as the Yasha monster rips the roof off a long tan edifice and lets out a roar that makes the ground shake. Then she reaches inside, and as she stands back upright, Shuri can see three people clutched in her giant hand. They all look too shocked to scream, but then the Yasha monster brings them up to eye level and roars again. Into their faces.

There is definitely some screaming now.

"You doubt my capabilities!" the Yasha monster shouts in a voice that sounds like a chorus of tortured ghouls.

And then she eats them.

By the time Shuri wakes the following morning, groggy and with an aching back from all the tossing and turning, she is so furious about this Yasha thing invading her subconscious, she's ready to scream herself.

"You did not sleep restfully," comes a voice from her left.

Shuri startles so forcefully, she falls off the bed. "Oww!"

"I have been told of your aim to attend a political forum with T'Challa," the voice continues. "You are not yet ready, Panther Cub."

Panther Cub . . .

"M'Shindi?" Shuri scrambles to her feet while simultaneously adjusting the wrap around her hair. It's always lopsided when she first wakes. "What are you doing here in my chambers?"

"That is, *Kocha* M'Shindi," the tiny old woman says from her perch on Shuri's window seat. "And I am here to observe."

"You were watching me *sleep*?" Shuri blurts, unable to contain her incredulity.

"Indeed. A trainee's rest patterns reveal infinitely more than a perfect punch or exquisitely executed blade swing. I said it before and will say it again: You, my dear, are most burdened."

The princess can do nothing but scowl.

"Dress," the Kocha says, rising to her feet.

"Dress?" *Like an* actual *dress?*

"In your training attire. We have much to accomplish."

"But—" *I haven't even woken* up *yet!* Shuri wants to shout.

But she doesn't. Because the Kocha hits her with a glare that could liquefy gold.

"Yes, Kocha," she says with an irresistible bow.

Then she scampers into her closet, planning to leave all thoughts of Yasha on the floor with her nightclothes.

Shuri spends the next twenty minutes so focused on walking with poise beside *the* Kocha, she doesn't deduce their destination until they are standing right outside it.

"Wait . . ." Shuri says, coming to a halt. Her eyes trace over the dusty, nondescript stone building. It's two stories high and the color of wet sand. Remarkable only for its lack of remarkability in comparison with the glisten and pomp of typical Wakandan architecture.

There is one thing of note: Above the glass double doors is a symbol—the red-green-and-black flag of Wakanda, with a pair of sharp-tipped spears crossed over it.

At that moment, a pair of uniformed Dora Milaje exit the building.

Their headquarters.

"You brought me to *Upanga*?"

"It would appear so," the Kocha says.

M'Shindi lifts a hand in a quick wave to the two women, and they smile at her before bowing their heads in greeting to Shuri. "Good morning, Your Majesty," one of them says.

"Uhh . . . good morning!" the princess replies with a tad too much enthusiasm. As soon as they're out of earshot, she turns to the short, older woman. "Not to question your destination choices, Kocha, but what are we doing here?"

"You," she says, "are here to learn. Come." And she takes off toward the entrance on her eerily silent feet. (The princess still hasn't been able to deduce how the Kocha moves so quietly without Vibranium. Because her footwear doesn't contain any. Shuri sneaked and checked with the miniature alien-metal detector she invented.)

The tiny woman is halfway to the doors by the time Shuri realizes *she's* still rooted to the spot.

"Wait!" She rushes to catch up. Once she does and the way inside looms larger, she could swear her heart flat-out quits its job. "Am I even *allowed* in there?" she whispers as the Kocha reaches for the door handle.

M'Shindi freezes. And turns.

Icy invisible fingers wend their way down Shuri's spine.

"So you invite yourself on a journey to a *different* nation, but feel discomfort at the notion of entering a building within the land you are first in line to rule?"

Well, when she puts it like that . . . (Touché, Kocha.)

M'Shindi opens the door, and they cross the threshold. Shuri is . . . surprised at the sparseness of the interior. Especially considering how ornate the Dora Milaje uniforms are. Half of the building is one big, open space with a sunken floor—three steps down— that contains a series of foam-padded sparring squares.

They remind Shuri of floor-level boxing rings with no ropes.

The other half of the building is split into two stories, and based on the breathless, sweating women going up the stairs, and the refreshed-looking ones coming down, Shuri would guess there's a place to bathe. Is that where the warriors live and sleep while off-duty?

Along the far wall are various weapons—scythes, spears, the signature rings Nakia prefers. (A glorified Frisbee with no middle and a knife's edge? The princess was petrified learning to wield one.)

"Whoa," Shuri says.

"Effective straightaway, you will train four days per week with the Dora Milaje candidates," comes M'Shindi's voice, cutting into Shuri's awe.

Her newly muscled body goes hot as her eyes bounce between the sparring squares. In two of them, pairs of well-toned girls a few years Shuri's senior are engaged in combat—with *very* sharp-looking weapons. And in a third, a group of twelve identically dressed girls moves through some type of drill in perfectly formed ranks. K'Marah is among them.

"Uhhh . . ."

"*KHUSELA!*" comes a collective shout from the group of twelve as they simultaneously shift into a wide-legged stance and cross their arms over their chests in a show of communal strength that makes the princess's heart swell with pride. She and K'Marah lock eyes, and the Dora-in-training nods in welcome.

But something is off with Shuri's best friend.

In fact, during their first round of one-on-one sparring—with all the other trainees watching on—Shuri manages not only to dodge one of K'Marah's strikes, but also to wedge a shoulder into her friend's midsection, flip her, and get her pinned.

Within less than a minute.

The whispers start almost immediately: "Wow!"

"Did you *see* that?"

"Pretty princess got *moves*!"

"Did Mining Queen just get owned??"

"She sure did. Bet that'll teach her a thing or two . . ."

Not sure what else to do, Shuri reaches a hand down to help her best friend up off the floor. "Good job," K'Marah says as she stands. But she won't look at the princess.

So of course, that's all Shuri can think about as she and K'Marah stand side by side watching the remaining matchups with the rest of the group: What could be wrong with the strongest, brightest girl Shuri knows?

Did K'Marah allow Shuri to win the match so she wouldn't be embarrassed in front of the others? Is K'Marah upset about Shuri training with *her* people? Yes, she and K'Marah spar all the time in Shuri's private sessions with M'Shindi and sometimes Okoye (which . . . is odd, now that Shuri thinks about it), but does the *real* Dora-in-training feel slighted by the princess being allowed to invade her space?

A sniff jolts Shuri from her ponderings, and she turns her head just in time to see K'Marah swipe at her eyes.

Now she's *really* worried.

"K'Marah," she whispers, facing back forward. "Are you—?"

"Shhh," the other girl replies. "Later."

Shuri practically holds her breath through the final handful of matches, and the moment the presiding Dora says, "You all are dismissed," Shuri rounds on her friend.

"I can leave and not return to train here if you'd prefer," she says (despite knowing she probably can't).

K'Marah sighs and shakes her head. "It's not that."

"So what is it—?"

Shuri stops speaking as she watches K'Marah's face morph into a mask of determined confidence. Which is when the princess realizes the presiding Dora is headed in their direction. "Excellent job today, Your Majesty," the woman says.

Shuri's face goes hot. "Thank you."

"K'Marah," the woman goes on, "I expect that whatever has broken your focus will be resolved before your arrival to this building tomorrow morning?"

K'Marah nods, resolute. "Yes, madam. My apologies."

"You ladies have a restful evening."

She walks away, and the girls continue toward the exit, in silence this time. Shuri can't bring herself to say anything else. Especially knowing that admonition likely hit her friend much harder than she's letting on. K'Marah has told Shuri before that she often struggles in Dora training because many of the others think her too frivolous and distractible. Now the princess has seen that hint of disdain from the others with her own eyes.

As they head back to the palace on foot, K'Marah takes occasional peeks over her shoulder. And it doesn't escape the princess's notice that her friend visibly relaxes the second they can no longer see Upanga.

After a few meters more, K'Marah stops completely.

And bursts into tears.

"Oh, Shuri!" she says, dropping her face into her hands.

Oh boy, the princess thinks.

"It's *awful*, Shuri."

"What is?"

K'Marah takes a steadying breath and then launches into . . . quite the tale: "Okay, so I have this friend, Josephine. She's French. I met her some time ago at this Global Summit on Advanced Tech your brother attended as the guest of the prime minister of Uganda. She did this super-cool presentation on some proto-type for these 'smart' prosthetic things that somehow regrow whatever limb they're being used to replace—"

"Wait . . . *really*??"

"Yes, but don't interrupt. I haven't gotten to the important part," K'Marah says. "Josephine's partner on the project was her cousin, Celeste. I've video-chatted with her a few times while talking to Jo, and she's really great, but Celeste wasn't at the summit because she got invited to some *other* tech thingy in Germany. Anyway . . . Josephine called me this morning and told me that Celeste is missing!"

Shuri's ears *really* perk up then. "Come again?"

"Jo hasn't been able to reach her in days! And they usually talk at *least* three to four times during each twenty-four-hour period. Jo said that the last time she spoke to Celeste, Celeste mentioned getting invited to something *else*, but she wouldn't tell Josephine pre-cisely what or where. It caused quite the rift between them. Anyway, the grown-ups keep brushing Jo off about the whole thing, but she's *sure* something is wrong, and I believe her."

"Yasha is missing, too," Shuri says before she can think better of it.

And she instantly regrets it.

"You mean that snooty girl we met in Kenya?" K'Marah says. "Holy Bast! They have to be connected!"

"Honestly, they don't," Shuri says, beginning to walk again. This conversation is making her feel like tiny, multi-legged creatures are crawling all over her. "I'm sure I spoke too soon," she calls back over her shoulder. "It's possible—likely even—that Yasha is merely ill."

"But what if she *isn't*, Shuri?" K'Marah says as she catches up and falls into step beside the princess.

Shuri shakes her head. "Even *if* she isn't, the statistical probability of there being a connection between two 'missing' girls from countries that are thousands of kilometers apart and don't share an official language is close to zero."

"But, Shuri—"

"They're not connected, K'Marah," Shuri says, ignoring a flash in her mind of her nightmare. Yasha eating people and the sudden bloom of dread behind her navel. "I'm sorry to hear about your friend's cousin, but there's not a whole lot *we* can do, is there?"

K'Marah sighs again. "No. I guess there isn't."

"Right. So let's get back to business. I have assessments to ace, and *you* need to refocus so that one instructor doesn't bite your head off again."

"Speaking of which," K'Marah says, "I totally let you win that match. Couldn't have the others thinking you're some weakling." She nudges Shuri with an elbow.

"Oh, how benevolent of you." Shuri rolls her eyes—maybe a *little* disappointed—and shoves her friend back.

And they continue on to the palace without exchanging another word.

4

HACKED

Shuri talks K'Marah into practicing some hand-and-foot drills once they reach her chambers, and neither girl says anything more about their "missing" acquaintances.

But Shuri can't stop thinking about it no matter how hard she tries.

A paragraph on dictatorships in her Global Political Systems textbook triggers highly disconcerting thoughts of Yasha being kidnapped, held hostage, and used to create some kind of environmental weapon of mass destruction. Which does it for the princess: She decides to go to the one place she *knows* she can focus—her lab.

In truth, it's been a while since she's spent any time there. Having a grown-up hovering nearby around the clock can really put a damper on a girl's sense of wonder and will to experiment.

Tonight, though, Shuri is desperate for a *real* distraction. So she grabs some study materials, and she and Nakia (Ayo has the night off) make their way to what the princess *hopes* is still her Zen zone.

And, thank Bast, it works. When her palm lands on the cool surface of the security scanner, she feels like lightning has shot through her veins. It makes her downright giddy. She bounces on her toes as the glass door slides open and the automated greeting fills the small cavern that serves as an entryway, then bursts into the foyer-like central space, drops to her knees, and presses her forehead to the gleaming floor. It sends a blissful chill over her neck, shoulders, and back.

Nakia's delighted laugher rings out behind the princess. "Guessing you missed this place?" she says.

"You have no idea," Shuri replies without lifting her head.

"Well, I guess I'll leave you to it. Ninety minutes sound okay?"

Wait . . .

Shuri sits up and looks over her shoulder at the uniform-clad guard. There's a conspiratorial spark in her eyes. "*Leave* me to it?" the princess says.

At this, Nakia smiles, and Shuri can see why T'Challa is smitten—Shuri used this fact against him to buy herself some time to leave the country when trying to save the heart-shaped herb, though he won't shoot his shot, the coward. "I will have a word with the queen mother. She'll understand."

And with a wink and a small bow, the Dora—who is *officially* Shuri's favorite now—turns around and takes her leave.

There's an alarm going off.

Shuri bolts upright, and something heavy falls from her lap without making a sound.

She jumps to her feet in a panic, trying to get her bearings, and there's a *thud* and CRASH behind her that make her whip around and land in Kocha M'Shindi's signature fighting stance: hands fisted and arms up, one guarding the face and ready to strike, the other guarding the body and ready to block; legs shoulder-width apart, with the dominant foot slightly behind the plant foot, and knees soft and ready to spring.

Her eyes land on an overturned little lab table, its former contents—a microscope slide holder, box of gears, and two conical flasks—scattered across the floor (by some miracle, only one of the flasks is broken).

And there's the wheeled chair that knocked the table over. It's the same chair Shuri plopped down into when she came into this lab station. On the floor at her feet? The mango-size and -shaped hunk of raw Vibranium she was examining while she studied a list of known properties.

She smacks her forehead. No idea when or how much time has elapsed since, but the princess clearly fell asleep.

And that annoying alarm is still going.

She looks around for the source of the slightly muffled noise. Her Kimoyo card is faceup on the desk at the back of this particular lab station, but the screen is black.

Shuri walks out into the open space of the foyer, and the sound gets louder. It's coming from the lab station to her right, and as she gets closer, she realizes that there's also a mechanized voice. "*Warning: intruder alert,*" says a robot-sounding woman every few seconds. It's coming from Shuri's desktop computer, which is perched on a steel table at the opposite end of the station, and faced away from her.

"*Warning: intruder alert . . .*"

She approaches slowly, gripped by the same sense of foreboding she felt when her Kimoyo card alerted her to that P.R.O.W.L. network ping yesterday afternoon. Except the closer she gets to her computer, the more the bad feeling intensifies . . . an alert on a system she *designed* to alert her to things is way different from a—

"*Warning: intruder alert . . .*"

Once she gets around to where she can see the screen, Shuri gasps. The cursor is moving around and things are clicking and windows are opening and words are appearing in search bars and results are populating—

Shuri is being hacked. For the span of a looooong beat, she just stands there. Staring. Because she can't believe it. Being hacked would mean someone managed to get through the complex system of firewalls, two-factor authentications, and encryptions the princess built with her own fingertips. And it has to be a some*one*—there's not an AI on earth who could override *her* cyber defenses.

"*Warning: intruder alert . . .*"

"Impossible . . ." she breathes into the air.

But it clearly *is* possible. Because as Shuri stands there agape, the transcript about Yasha's absence from the lab in Kenya appears on the screen, scrolls of its own accord, then zooms and latches on to the phrase *no call, no show*.

The virtual intruder has accessed the P.R.O.W.L. network.

Shuri leaps into action. After disabling the alarm (*so* annoying, that noise and voice), she decides the only viable course of action is to . . . hack back. Yes, she could cut her Internet connection to kick the interloper out, but the princess knows that if they got in once, they'll get in again.

Also: This isn't just about her now. Sensitive information from other nations, including the one run by Ororo—weather goddess, mistress of the elements, and all-around mutant super heroine—is now vulnerable. Which makes Shuri feel a mixture of furious and petrified. She is *sure* she had the surveillance network locked down tighter than that polygon place in America that holds all the nation's secrets. Managing to break into it would mean that the intruder has tech skills far above and beyond even the princess's. In the wrong hands, information acquired through P.R.O.W.L. could be used to wreak havoc of international proportions.

Shuri has to find out who this hacker is before they can cause Wakandan allies—or Wakanda itself—any harm.

She runs back to the other lab station to grab her laptop and quickly hops onto the network. The hack back is much easier than the princess anticipates: Whoever broke through left their *own* network wide open (which seems amateurish?).

Shuri slips right in.

And she has to move fast. There's a good chance that the moment Shuri's presence is detected, her intruder will pull the plug and end the connection.

As quickly as she can, Shuri activates the trespasser's webcam (again: rookie move leaving it uncovered; this hacker is either wildly *over*confident or not nearly as stealthy as a *good* hacker should be).

And instantly draws back.

It's a girl. *Maybe* Shuri's age, but certainly no older. Brown-skinned with short, curly hair cut sort of asymmetrically. She's so focused on the stuff she's poking through on Shuri's other computer, she hasn't realized she's literally being watched.

This girl needs a lesson in snooping.

While she continues opening windows and scanning through what she finds—curly girl is now combing through a bunch of French newspapers (is this girl French?)—Shuri decides to do some digging of her own.

What she discovers? In addition to being a similar age—she's a twelve-year-old high schooler (which

Shuri didn't realize was possible) in the American city of Chicago—similar complexion, and similarly computer savvy, the hacker extraordinaire *also* has a name that ends in "ri": Riri. Surname "Williams."

And despite the fact that Riri's a total stranger, Shuri relaxes the slightest bit. Based on what she's seen in the girl's own files, most of which are related to schoolwork, it's highly unlikely that this Riri's hacking motives are malicious.

There are a few strange schematics for what looks like some sort of metal super suit, but if the girl is anything like Shuri—and the princess suspects that she is—it's nothing more than a fun side experiment. So what is she after?

"Guess there's one way to find out . . ." Shuri says before taking a deep breath and establishing a web call.

She leaves her camera off at first. "Umm, hello?" she says once she can hear Riri muttering under her breath. "Riri, is it?"

The girl jolts so forcefully, her chair topples backward. She disappears from the frame, crashing to the floor with a yelp. After a few seconds, the top of her head comes into view, and then her eyes. Which look like they've seen the undead and aren't sure if *she's* still alive to tell about it.

"Ahh . . . yes. I am the owner of the network you've infiltrated," Shuri continues. *How strange it must be to hear some disembodied voice who knows your name coming out of your computer.* "Explain yourself, young lady."

Shuri watches Riri's eyes flick left, then come back. *She's about to unplug.*

"Wait! Don't disconnect! I'm—" *Just like you,* Shuri wants to say but doesn't. Someone with harmful intentions could say the same thing. Shuri certainly wouldn't believe it if it were said to *her.*

She huffs. There's only one thing to do.

After a quick glance in the thick-paned glass of the wall behind her to make sure her hair looks okay, Shuri launches her own webcam.

"Hi," she says to Riri with a wave.

Riri's eyebrows rise before she does, but when Shuri doesn't vanish—or morph into some many-headed monster—the younger girl rights her chair and replants herself in front of her computer screen. Mouth agape.

It makes Shuri giggle. "I felt the same way when I first saw *you,*" she says.

"Who *are* you?" Riri replies, awe dancing all over her face. It makes Shuri feel . . . like she really *matters.* (Does T'Challa get to feel this way all the time?)

But also: How should she respond? Admitting to

being the princess of a hidden nation in Africa doesn't seem the way to go no matter how young and innocent this Riri looks. "Well . . ." Shuri says, deciding to take the "bad cop" route, "I don't really think you're at liberty to ask me that question. Who are *you*, and why did you hack me?"

"Uhhh . . ." Riri's eyes dart around as though seeking an escape route.

"And don't even think about lying," Shuri continues. "I have pinned your location and will alert the authorities to your activities." This isn't the least bit true, but this Riri character couldn't possibly know that.

Or could she? "Hmm . . ." Riri's eyes narrow and her head cocks to one side. "Not to burst your bubble or anything, but based on stuff I found on *your* network, I'd say *you'd* be the one in trouble with the 'authorities.' In, like . . . eleven different countries. That surveillance network you built is epic, but also, like, *super* illegal. I was expecting you to be some world-domination-plotting white dude who lives in his mom's basement with a stockpile of weapons."

Shuri can't help but laugh. She kind of likes this Riri. "Fine," she says, deciding on a different tactic. "Tell me why you infiltrated my network or I'll wipe your entire system, and you'll have to spend hours retrieving it all from backups. Which, if you're any-thing like me, are all on external hard drives."

Riri gasps. "You wouldn't."

"Oh, I most certainly would. Especially considering how much you've seen."

For the space of a few seconds, neither girl speaks.

Then Riri deflates. "My friend is missing," she says. "I only found *you* because I'm looking for *her*."

MISSION LOG

**THE FOLLOWING TRANSCRIPT IS A CONVER-
SATION BETWEEN TWELVE-YEAR-OLD RIRI
WILLIAMS (WHO MANAGED TO HACK MY NETWORK
DESPITE IT SURELY BEING ONE OF THE MOST
SECURE ON THE PLANET, NOT TO TOOT MY OWN
HORN) OF CHICAGO, USA, AND ME.**

Full disclosure: I began recording just
after she shared that a girl she knows
has gone missing . . . and no one seems
to notice but Riri.

ME: . . . OKAY, I'M BACK. CAN YOU REPEAT THAT?
RIRI: I SAID, I ONLY FOUND YOU—WELL, FOUND
YOUR NETWORK—BECAUSE I WAS LOOKING
FOR HER.
ME: TELL ME MORE.

RIRI: (AUDIBLE PAUSE) FINE, BUT WILL YOU HEAR ME OUT ALL THE WAY BEFORE YOU RESPOND?

ME: I CAN AGREE TO THAT.

RIRI: OKAY. THANK YOU. (AUDIBLE SIGH) THE LONG AND SHORT OF IT IS THAT I HAVE THIS … ACQUAINTANCE. I WOULDN'T CALL US FRIENDS, PER SE. I DON'T REALLY HAVE MANY OF THOSE SINCE MY BEST FRIEND, NATALIE, WAS—(AUDIBLE PAUSE) NEVER MIND. ANYWAY, THIS GIRL'S NAME IS CICI, AND PEOPLE WOULD CONSTANTLY GET US CONFUSED BECAUSE OUR NAMES RHYME AND WE WERE THE ONLY TWO BLACK GIRLS IN THIS SUM-MER ROBOTICS PROGRAM AT THE UNIVERSITY HERE. SHE'S SUPER SMART LIKE ME, BUT A FEW YEARS OLDER. AND SHE LIVES DOWN THE ROAD, SO I SEE HER ALL THE TIME ON THE WAY TO AND FROM SCHOOL EVEN THOUGH WE DON'T REALLY TALK. SHE DOESN'T HAVE FRIENDS, EITHER, BUT WE MAKE EYE CONTACT SOMETIMES, AND I FEEL LIKE SHE SORTA LOOKS OUT FOR ME? HARD BEING A TWELVE-YEAR-OLD HIGH SCHOOLER, LEMME TELL YA. SHE'S LIKE THIS PSEUDO BIG SISTER.

WHICH IS WHY I KNOW SOMETHING IS WRONG. I HAVEN'T SEEN HER IN FOUR DAYS. AND I HAVE THIS … HUNCH, I GUESS. THAT SHE'S IN

TROUBLE. THAT SHE'S MISSING IN THE FOUL-PLAY
SENSE OF THE WORD?

ME: SO—

RIRI: I'M NOT DONE! GIMME, LIKE, ONE MORE MIN-
UTE. THE OTHER THING IS THAT A WEEK AND A
HALF AGO, THIS STRANGE WOMAN WEARING A
SKIRT SUIT AND CARRYING A CLIPBOARD TRIED TO
TALK TO ME AS I WALKED HOME FROM THE BUS
STOP. THE STRANGER-DANGER VIBES WERE
STRONG, SO I SKEDADDLED. ANYONE WHO
CAN STAND, LET ALONE WALK, IN THE POINTY-
TOE, SKY-HIGH HEELS SHE WAS WEARING HAS TO
BE UP TO NO GOOD, AM I RIGHT?

ME: I WOU—

RIRI: WELL, FIVE DAYS AGO, I SAW CICI TALKING TO
THAT SAME LADY. AND I HAVEN'T SEEN HER—
THEM: CICI OR THE LADY—SINCE. I EVEN WENT TO
HER HOUSE TODAY AND NO ONE ANSWERED THE
DOOR. THERE WAS A LIGHT ON INSIDE, SO I
KNOW SOMEONE WAS IN THERE …

ME: HOL—

RIRI: WE DON'T JUST LEAVE LIGHTS ON AROUND
HERE. "THESE BILLS DON'T PAY THEMSELVES," AS MY
MOM CONSTANTLY REMINDS ME, AND—

ME: RIRI!

RIRI: HUH?

ME: I DON'T MEAN TO RUSH YOU, BUT DO YOU THINK YOU COULD GET TO THE PART WHERE YOU DECIDED TO HACK ME?

RIRI: OH. YEAH, OKAY. WELL, I WAS ON THE WEB TRYING TO FIND OUT IF ANYONE HAS REPORTED CICI MISSING—NO ONE HAS ... THOUGH THAT'S SADLY NOT UNCOMMON WHEN IT COMES TO GIRLS LIKE US AROUND HERE. SO THEN I STARTED LOOKING INTO OTHER MISSING-GIRLS CASES THAT *HAVE* BEEN REPORTED WITHIN THE PAST MONTH, AND THAT LED ME TO A "GIRLS IN STEM" MESSAGE BOARD ABOUT THIS GIRL NAMED KATHERINE PRYDE WHO IS MISSING FROM DEERFIELD, A SUBURB NOT TOO FAR FROM HERE, AND ON THAT MESSAGE BOARD THERE WAS MENTION OF KATHERINE DEVELOPING A LONG-DISTANCE FRIENDSHIP WITH A GIRL IN THE PHILIPPINES ... WHO ALSO TURNED UP MISSING.

ME: WHOA.

RIRI: YEAH. SO I FOUND KATHERINE'S SCREEN NAME AND THE SCREEN NAME OF THE GIRL FROM THE PHILIPPINES, AND WENT IN AND CHECKED THEIR CHAT HISTORIES AND ANY MUTUAL FRIENDS. WHICH LED ME TO A GIRL WHO'D BEEN CHATTING WITH BOTH OF THEM FROM KENYA.

ON A HUNCH, I WENT INTO THE NETWORK THE
KENYAN GIRL USED TO ACCESS THE MESSAGE
BOARD. THAT'S WHERE I FOUND A SURVEILLANCE
BUG I KNEW SHOULDN'T BE THERE—
ME: MINE.
RIRI: YOURS. IT SEEMED MALICIOUS, THE SORT OF
CYBER-SPYING YOU'VE GOT GOING ON. SO I
DECIDED TO HACK IN AND SEE WHAT I COULD
FIND—

    END TRANSCRIPTION.

The entryway buzzer sounded at that
point—Nakia returning to escort me back
to the palace—but I'd certainly heard
enough. That "malicious" comment aside
(I am merely looking out for the best
interests of my country, thank you very
much), there is now no denying the possibility of a . . . correlation between
these apparent disappearances.

Though I'm not entirely sure what to do
about it. Telling Mother and T'Challa
seems counterintuitive—especially considering that (a) I'm supposed to be preparing
for my upcoming assessments, and (b) I'd
have to reveal my surveillance network to

them (Riri wasn't wrong about it maybe getting me into some trouble).

Besides, what would *they* do about it? It isn't as though we have any definitive evidence that the "disappearances" are connected. And there remains the fact that no alarms have been sounded. No authorities alerted. No parents/guardians reporting their girls "missing."

I've asked Riri to keep me updated with regard to her missing acquaintance, but I'm going to get back to my studies.

Well . . . after I retool my encryption system and strengthen my firewalls. Girl genius or not, being hacked again (and so easily!) is *not* on my to-be-accomplished list.

5

DISTRACTION

But of course, the princess can't let it go. She checks in with Riri every eight hours over the next two days, and sets the P.R.O.W.L. system to run a keyword scan every hour on the hour.

And the results are staggering. There are multiple message boards like the one Riri stumbled upon, and taken together, they reveal a troubling phenomenon: Around the world, girls aged ten to fifteen—all notably accomplished in science, technology, engineering, and mathematics fields—have gone missing. But no one seems to notice (or care?) besides . . . other girls.

There's a physics prodigy—her award-winning research on quarks sparked a national discourse— missing in Bolivia. The robotics genius who created a rover capable of exploring the surface of Jupiter is missing in South Africa. In addition to her work in prosthetics, the cousin of K'Marah's French friend also won an innovator prize for coding. There's a girl missing in Pakistan who, using a high-powered telescope she scavenged from an observatory destroyed in a fire, discovered an entire planetary system in a neighboring galaxy.

And on and on and on.

But despite how distracted she's become with the matter, Shuri has yet to puzzle out a viable course of action. It's impossible to *prove* the disappearances are connected, and since there haven't been any official reports of the missing girls (she's checked every police system she could get into), Shuri and Riri both know that without any real evidence of foul play, no adults are going to take them seriously.

It's frustrating, to say the very least.

The one person she does let in on her secret surveilling? K'Marah.

"Whoa," the Dora-in-training says when Shuri gives her a quick tour of the P.R.O.W.L. on the open laptop in Shuri's closet mini-laboratory. "This is . . . extensive."

While she'd never admit it, Shuri's been desperate to tell *someone* about the things she and Riri have discovered. And while K'Marah can be a bit dramatic, there's no denying how helpful she was to the princess during the heart-shaped herb crisis. It's not the same, of course, but it is a relief to share the burden of this particular mystery.

Not that K'Marah is *helpful* at all.

"So," she says, turning to Shuri after scanning the information. "What are we going to do?"

"Do?"

"Umm . . . yeah. We have to do *something*, Shuri. These girls are clearly in danger."

"I mean, let's not be rash," Shuri replies in her best grown-up voice. "Firstly, we don't *know* they're in danger. I know at a glance, all this *seems* suspicious and connected, but there are something like half a billion adolescent girls on Earth, and in the United States *alone*, approximately two thousand children go missing every day. Riri and I looked up the statistics—"

"Who *cares* about 'statistics,' Shuri? These girls need our help—"

"But we don't *know* that for sure, K'Marah!" Shuri gulps, forcing herself to put conviction behind her words. "We can't. That's what I'm trying to tell you." The princess squats to pick up a rogue slipper and return it to its mate . . . at the opposite end of the dressing chamber. "All these 'disappearances' might *look* connected, but there's actually a higher probability of . . . coincidence. Is all I'm saying."

When K'Marah doesn't immediately respond, Shuri turns to make sure she was heard. K'Marah cocks her elaborately braided head to one side and examines Shuri's face the way she would an enemy of the state under Dora Milaje interrogation. The princess fights to hold her friend's gaze—she's spent enough time training with the prestigious guards to know exactly what K'Marah is doing—but after mere seconds, her eyes drop.

"Ah-ha!" K'Marah says.

Shuri turns away. "What?"

"You don't believe your own words."

"Yes, I do—"

"No. You don't. You know just as well as I do that despite your *probabilities* or whatever the heck you calculated, there is no way these kidnappings aren't linked."

"They may not be kidnappings!" Shuri shouts. But she sounds silly even to herself now. Kidnappings or not, K'Marah—and Riri, for that matter—is right: The disappearances *feel* connected. Despite the low odds. Really, the fact that *none* of them have been reported is in itself more than a bit suspect. Riri also shared statistics about high rates of unreported disappearances among underprivileged girls of color in "urban" American landscapes, but is the same true in the other nations where girls have gone missing?

K'Marah smirks at the princess in that *way* she does when she knows that Shuri knows she (K'Marah) is right.

"And anyway," Shuri goes on, shutting the laptop with a snap, "even if they were kidnappings—and I am *not* saying they are!—we can't *prove* it. We have no evidence! No real leads. I have nothing at all that would help us with any sort of search."

"We have names," K'Marah says resolutely. "Quite a few of them."

"Okay . . . And?"

"And . . . well . . . I mean, we can . . ."

Now Shuri's the one grinning. Which does feel a tad inappropriate considering the topic of conversation, but there is something satisfying about seeing K'Marah's surety slip. "Told ya," the princess says, with a shrug. "No matter how much you, Riri, or I *want* to get to the bottom of this, we're all severely limited with regard to actions we can actually take."

"Fine."

Sweet victory. (And though Shuri would never admit it: relief.)

"The least you could do is feed the names into your little global surveillance thingy." K'Marah gestures toward Shuri's now-closed computer.

And all the oxygen vanishes from the air around Shuri's head.

It hits her: She doesn't *want* the disappearances to be connected. Saving some plants—and by extension, her homeland—was one thing. This? Girls vanishing without a trace all over the *world*? This feels . . . different. The princess hasn't even successfully completed her Panther training. A thing she needs to do in order to *continue* protecting her homeland—by accompanying T'Challa to that tech conclave.

For the first time in a long time, Shuri can *feel* how young she is.

What happens if she inputs the names . . . and gets a hit on one (or more!) of them? Then she'll have to take some sort of action, won't she? And what if . . . it's more than the princess is distinctly prepared for?

"Well?" K'Marah is saying. "You gonna put that 'system' of yours to use in an honorable way? Or have you gone all digital spy for no *good* reason?"

Shuri scowls. "Fine," she says. She lifts her arm and taps a Kimoyo bead. *09:52* appears in midair in glowing purple above her wrist. "But it'll have to wait. We're about to be late for training."

"Oh my goodness!" K'Marah says, scrambling around the pullout table and bolting toward the exit. She almost trips over the train of a shimmering indigo gown Shuri has zero intention of ever wearing. "I can-*not* be late again! Okoye will have my head!"

As the sound of K'Marah's fleeing footsteps fades, Shuri exhales, thankful for her friend's distraction. But then her gaze is drawn to the closed computer, and the relief evaporates like dew off a glowing heart-shaped herb petal at dawn.

Because Shuri is distracted, too.

6

REFOCUS

Very, very distracted.

Though K'Marah manages to partially regain her focus, Shuri's performance during her training with the Dora Milaje leaves much to be desired. And the other girls begin to take notice.

After one particularly dismal sparring session, K'Marah pulls her aside. "I don't know what has gotten into you, Princess, but you have to snap out of it." She sneaks a peek to the right, and when Shuri follows her eyes, her throat practically closes: Kocha M'Shindi is standing against a far wall. "She's been watching your every move," K'Marah continues. "I overheard one of the older girls say word of your . . . *retrogression*—I believe that's the term she used—is making its way around. No clue whether or not that's true, but perhaps you should *act* as though it is. The last thing *you* need is for the queen mother to hear you're not excelling here." She gives Shuri a knowing look.

And despite understanding how right K'Marah is, Shuri also feels a surge of anger toward this best friend of hers. Prior to K'Marah making a huge deal of the so-called kidnappings of all those girls, Shuri was doing just fine. Now, in addition to the unavoidable little reminders of the missing girls, she's racked with a gnawing sense of guilt. Because she still hasn't *done* anything. Nothing for the girls, at least.

She *did* re-secure the P.R.O.W.L. network and implement a counterattack measure that will unleash a highly destructive virus on any attempted intruder's operating system. But Shuri has yet to add the names of the other girls to the P.R.O.W.L.'s hit list.

Which is another reason this conversation with K'Marah is intensely discomfiting. As the clearly concerned shorter girl looks up into Shuri's face, all the princess can really think is, *Great Bast, please don't let her ask if there have been any hits on the girls' names.*

Distracted.

"Helloooo? Wakanda to Shuri?" K'Marah taps Shuri's nose, and the princess snaps back to where she's standing on the shock-absorbent foam floor of a sparring circle inside Upanga. A place she thought she'd only ever see from the outside.

Opportunity of a lifetime, and she's too distracted to make the most of it. "Huh?"

"I asked if you wanted to meet later and go over some drills," K'Marah says. "I won't throw any more of our matches to make you look good, but I'm willing to help a sister out."

"Mmmm . . ." As tempting as the offer is, Shuri is 100 percent sure the vanished-girl-genius mystery will come up if she spends any time with K'Marah outside this training facility. "I appreciate it, *sis*. But I think I should get some rest. Could use a reboot—I mean . . ."

Shuri realizes her mistake. *Curse this tech-term-filled brain of mine!* she thinks.

"Hey, speaking of *reboot* . . ." K'Marah peeks around, then takes a half step closer to Shuri and lowers her voice. "Any news on . . . you know what? I'm sure you've rebooted *that* whole thing by now, right?"

"Oh, umm . . . yeah. I have," Shuri says. "But we shouldn't talk about that here." She tips her head toward the group of three older Dora trainees who have appeared to their left. Not that she's actually bothered by their sudden presence: It gives her an easy out.

"Ah," K'Marah says, stepping back. "Understood."

"Nothing new to report, anyway." Shuri yawns for effect. "I'm going to head back to the palace for a nap. Bast knows I could use one. We'll reconvene later?" The princess gives K'Marah a quick side hug and makes a dash for her stuff.

She tries not to notice the whispers of "*Must be nice*" from behind her. Or the feeling of Kocha M'Shindi's heavy gaze on her back as she goes.

Shuri really *must* be tired: The palace seems much farther away from Upanga than she remembers. The princess isn't sure exactly how long she's been walking, but the gilded watchtowers at the front corners of her home should be peeking over the horizon by now. The sun is also higher in the sky than she'd expect it to be this late in the afternoon. It's hot. Too hot. And also too quiet.

Shuri looks back over her shoulder to see if she's made any progress at all. She's gotten far enough away from the training facility for it to have disappeared from view but—

There's a flash of movement to her right, but when she looks, no one is there. Despite the heat, a chill creeps over Shuri's skin, making her feel as though there are spiders all over her scalp, crawling their way down her arms and legs. Which is when she realizes she's alone. Yes, she told K'Marah she wasn't up for hanging out—aka getting her butt kicked in her own sleeping chambers—but did she really leave Upanga with no escort whatsoever? Isn't Nakia supposed to be on duty right now?

There's another flash, to the left this time, and Shuri's head whips in that direction. "Who . . . who's there?"

Something grazes her arm, and she shifts into the signature Dora Milaje fighting stance. (Though she feels strange about it—it's certainly not a stance T'Challa would employ . . . Should she be using *different* moves? Like . . . special Panther ones?) "Show yourself," she commands. "By order of the princess."

There's an amused huff from behind her . . . which she feels more than hears: Who/whatever is stalking her is standing so close, its breath hits the back of her neck.

Quick as she can, Shuri drops into a squat, intending to rotate at the last second and use an outstretched leg to sweep the feet of her attacker out from under them. But the person—for the princess is certain it's a person now—anticipates the move and not only jumps at precisely the right moment, but manages to kick Shuri square in the chest on the way down, knocking the wind from her lungs.

"You've been distracted, Panther Cub," comes a

voice that is all too familiar. "It shows." A kick to her ribs makes Shuri's vision go white at the edges. "Such a shame. You had so much potential."

She has to fight back.

She can sense another kick coming (how? she has no idea), so she rolls to her stomach just in time to avoid it, and then shoves up to her feet. Her head swims, but her attacker comes into focus: Kocha M'Shindi.

The older woman steps up to Shuri with her hands behind her back. Cool as an ice cube in a glass of mango nectar. "I am disappointed," she says. And then she strikes. Shuri blocks the blow aimed at her throat, but M'Shindi's other fist—tiny though it may be— lands home right above the princess's navel.

"Still struggling with dual-eyed defense, I see," M'Shindi taunts.

Then faster than Shuri can blink, the frail-looking woman has grabbed one of Shuri's arms, rotated to shove a shoulder into Shuri's midsection, and flipped Shuri over. Shuri lands on her back with a thud, and M'Shindi's knee comes down on Shuri's sternum to pin her.

"You've failed," she says, lowering her face to Shuri's and staring into the princess's eyes in that creepy way she does. "You've failed your Phase One assessments. Your distraction has cost you dearly—"

A pinging sound fills the air around Shuri's head.

Almost like it's coming from right beside her. She looks left and right, seeing nothing but dirt, but when she turns back to M'Shindi, ready to try and get the woman off her, she discovers *several* faces looking down at her. All vaguely familiar.

"I would've discovered life in a neighboring galaxy had you looked for me," comes the voice of one girl with medium-brown skin and straight, dark hair.

"And I was working on a cure for lupus," an East Asian girl chimes in.

"Why aren't you looking for us?" comes the voice of a Black American girl whose face Shuri *does* recognize: Riri's neighbor Cici.

The *ping* chimes again. Louder this time. Shuri shuts her eyes.

"You are far too distracted, Panther Cub." M'Shindi is back over her, breath on her face—

PING!

Shuri jolts awake and looks around, trying to get her bearings. She's seated in a tall, hard-backed chair at a lab table within a narrow room lined on both sides with jewel-toned clothing.

There's an open laptop in front of her.

PING!

She shakes her head to clear it, and a series of words come into focus on the computer screen.

BUG ALERT!
Location: Throne Room
Incident: Keyword "conclave"
Conversation in progress

That certainly gets Shuri's attention.

She scrambles to get the app open so she can listen in—

". . . RUMORED TO HAVE TIES TO KLAW."
"AND YOU STILL THINK IT WISE TO ATTEND, T'CHALLA?"
"IT IS VITAL THAT WE, AS ONE OF THE MOST TECHNOLOGICALLY ADVANCED NATIONS ON THE CONTINENT, ARE IN ATTENDANCE AT A MULTINATIONAL SUMMIT ON SECURITY-RELATED TECHNOLOGY. BESIDES, NO ONE KNOWS THAT I AM COMING, MOTHER. THE AMBASSADOR HAS ASSURED ME OF THAT."
"SECRECY IS NOT AN ASSURANCE OF SAFETY, MY DEAR. I WILL NOT CHALLENGE THE KING'S PRIORITIES OR DECISIONS, BUT IT WOULD BEHOOVE YOU TO CONSIDER WHETHER OR NOT THIS CONCLAVE IS THE PROPER PLACE TO ANNOUNCE YOUR INTENTIONS FOR THE NEAR FUTURE OF THIS NATION."

"WE MUSTN'T ALLOW FEAR TO DECIDE OUR PATHS, MOTHER. PERHAPS THIS IS AN OPPORTUNITY. ULYSSES KLAW MURDERED BABA AND HAS YET TO SUFFER ANY CONSE-QUENCES. YOU FEAR MY PRESENCE AT THIS GATHERING LEADING HIM BACK TO US, BUT CONSIDER THE POSSIBILITY THAT IT COULD LEAD ME TO HIM—"

"THIS IS NOT THE TIME FOR VENGEANCE, MY SON."

"I DO NOT DISAGREE. BUT LET US SEE WHAT TRANSPIRES . . ."

A message from Riri pops up:

> *Went to the front office at my school today to ask about Cici, and the aide let it slip that she got withdrawn. Went by her house again, and no one answered.*

Shuri sighs.

She *has* to get back on track. Train hard and "crush" (as she's heard K'Marah say) her assessments so she'll be permitted to attend the conclave with T'Challa, who is clearly insistent on attending no matter what. Knowing he'll be a single degree of separation from Ulysses Klaw . . . what if Klaw himself turns up there? He, like T'Challa, could also be planning a surprise appearance. Shuri *must* be there. Not because the Dora Milaje—K'Marah included—are ill-equipped for their jobs. It's just that the princess is first in line to the throne *and* she builds the tech. Which means she needs to become *more* equipped. Being directly privy to tech-related information *and* adding an extra pair of eyes watching T'Challa's back feel like "must-dos."

But when she blinks, the faces of those girls from her dream flash behind her eyelids. As much as the princess would *like* to pretend they don't exist, she can't.

With a shake of her head, Shuri opens her P.R.O.W.L. network settings and adds all the names she has memorized to her keyword list. There are seven in all. She tosses herself, K'Marah, and Riri in to round it out to ten.

Then she nods, shuts the computer, and grabs her knapsack before lifting her wrist to place a Kimoyo call.

"Hey, K'Marah," she says when the other girl's hologram appears above her arm. "So, about those drills . . ."

Floating K'Marah just grins. "I knew you'd change your mind," she says.

7

ASSESSED

The more time that passes without any alerts from the P.R.O.W.L. system, the more Shuri is able to drill down on what matters most (to her, at least): her studies and combat training.

Not that the renewed concentration does anything to quell her stress nightmares. She has a minimum of two per night, and they always involve failed evaluations, "missing" girls in varying states of either distress or fury, or a combination of both.

There's the one where everything she knows about her favorite sound-absorbing metal vanishes from her head the moment she sits down to take her History and Known Properties of Vibranium examination. Which is frustrating. Not only because she knows more about the stuff than 99.9999 percent of all other people on Earth, (she's only ever met one person who knows more, and the last time she saw *him*, he was pacing and muttering something about a cube in a low-lit dungeon-esque laboratory in London), but also because she achieved a perfect score on that exact examination hours *before* having the nightmare.

In another one, she can't get her arms or legs to move during a hand-to-hand combat test, and all the missing girls appear around her, pointing and laughing before they close in and move her limbs about like she's a mannequin while she tries (and fails) to scream. A variation of *that* one involves K'Marah taking her down in a sparring match and the girls all closing in on her before K'Marah kicks her in the ribs (which always wakes Shuri RIGHT up.) And there's one the morning of a timed test *involving* a mannequin where seven seconds in, Shuri realizes she's actually fighting Nakia and they're in the throne room with an audience: Mother, T'Challa, Uncle S'Yan, and the entire council of tribal elders. A good ol' Taifa Ngao with Shuri's evaluation as the reason for gathering.

On the bright side, the princess is typically able to shake off the shudder-inducing pseudo-circumstances once her eyes have opened, and though some of her scores don't wind up as *high* as she'd like for them to be, they are all above passing. And with each *Exceeds Expectations* comes a slight uptick in confidence: Bad dreams aside, perhaps she *does* have what it takes to eventually don a Vibranium-infused suit of her own and take on the Black Panther mantle—if it ever comes to that.

Shuri manages to get *so* focused, in fact, it completely escapes her notice that the more she improves, the more K'Marah seems to decline. It doesn't occur to the princess at all that her best friend is no longer at the top of her Dora trainee class—or even in the middle—until one of the rare nights Okoye is assigned to be her glorified babysitter at the lab, and the gorgeous (and lethal) general interrupts her intensive study session.

"Your Majesty?"

Shuri startles, and her Djalia 101 textbook topples to the gleaming resin floor.

"My apologies, Princess," Okoye says, retrieving the tome. "For the jolt as well as this drudgery." She hands the book back to Shuri, her face scrunched up as though the pages were covered in rhinoceros dung.

"Definitely my *least* favorite subject during my own years of schooling. Yeesh."

Shuri wants to laugh, but can't seem to get her chest to loosen. It's certainly not every day that the head of the Dora Milaje *and* Wakandan defensive forces speaks to her as though she's a friend.

It . . . makes Shuri nervous. Especially when the general's eyes scan the perimeter of the room before falling back on her. "Who, might I ask, has access to your laboratory's surveillance footage?"

"Umm . . . just me. There's a dual-authentication mechanism involving both a password and a retinal scan."

"Good," Okoye says with a single nod. "So I can trust that this conversation will stay between the two of us?"

Shuri gulps. "Yes, General."

"Wonderful. I would never want it said that I showed partiality toward a single Dora Milaje candidate because that is something I would certainly *not* do. But I am . . . *concerned* about a trainee I know you share a deep connection with."

This certainly isn't the direction Shuri expected the discussion to take. "Concerned?"

"Yes. Her performance as of late has left much to be desired. Especially considering . . . well, how far *ahead* of the others she was. I just wondered, between the two of us of course, if there is anything you feel I should . . . take into consideration."

The princess is too baffled to respond. But Okoye doesn't say anything more.

As the silence stretches—with the general staring at Shuri like the secret to world peace will spill from her mouth the moment she opens it—Shuri realizes she'll have to say *something*. What comes out when she finally does speak: "There is something wrong with K'Marah?"

"That is the question I hoped you could answer for *me*," Okoye replies. She sighs and shakes her head. "I am deeply fond of your dear friend, Shuri. She is full of promise. At her initial level of performance, she would have become one of the greatest Dora Milaje in the history of this great nation. And quickly. But as of late . . ." Her gaze drifts off.

Shuri hasn't the vaguest idea of what to say. It was one thing to overhear the older girls bad-mouthing K'Marah after she "lost" to Shuri in their first sparring match at Upanga. This, though? Has the princess really been so tuned out, she failed to notice her best friend floundering—again? Last she checked, K'Marah still managed to defeat *Shuri* in every match . . .

A telltale chime rings out from the desktop

computer in the center lab station, and Shuri freezes, eyes widening.

"Are you quite all right, Your Majesty?" Okoye looks in the direction of the little room, a cobra preparing to strike.

"Oh yes, yes!" Shuri says, her enthusiasm so forced it makes *her* cringe. "That's just . . . an alarm! Time is really flying, huh?" She gathers all the open books and scattered papers in front of her to return them to her knapsack. Then she stands. "We should head back to the palace now."

Because that chime? It means there's a new message from Riri. Shuri retooled her network settings so that the only device in the entire kingdom that can receive messages from Riri is that particular desktop computer. Aka the princess is spared any and all overly concerned contact from the American girl unless she happens to be here in the lab. It's also now the only device that can access the P.R.O.W.L. network.

And she wants to get away from it as quickly as possible.

"I'll check on K'Marah," Shuri says, breezing past the skeptical general to the laboratory exit. She's halfway up the cave-like corridor before she hears Okoye fall into line slightly behind and to her right.

For the entire seven-minute trip back to the palace

in the hovercar Shuri's mother insisted they take, neither the princess nor the general speaks.

True to her word, and in an effort to distract her from speculation about that message from Riri she can't bring herself to check—she has to stay *focused* on what she can control—Shuri does check on K'Marah. Who, as it turns out, is distraught for a valid reason: She hasn't been able to reach that French friend of hers in days.

"I'm sure you think I'm 'overreacting,'" the Dora-in-training says to Shuri through tears as they sit in Shuri's quarters eating a delivered breakfast the following morning, "but the last time I spoke to her, she was telling me about some lead on her missing cousin she intended to pursue. I just can't help but wonder if she discovered something she wasn't supposed to and—"

She doesn't finish the thought. She doesn't have to.

"Why didn't you tell me this, K'Marah?" Shuri says, surprising herself. In truth, she's . . . stung.

That sting becomes a burn when K'Marah snorts. "You've made it *very* clear that you think all this disappearing-girls stuff is a silly waste of time. I'd rather not be made to feel bad about being upset. Honestly not even sure why I'm telling you now." She sniffles and wipes her face on a billowing sleeve of the (slightly ludicrous) chartreuse robe thing she's wearing. Then she shifts to get up. "I should go."

"K'Marah, wait—"

"It's fine, Shuri," the departing girl says without slowing down. "And don't worry: I'll pull it together and get refocused on training. I'm sure that's the only reason you asked how I am, right?"

And with that, she's gone.

Shuri stares at the closed door, her mind spinning like an Ororo-generated hurricane. She can't figure out what to say—not that there's anybody to say anything *to*—or what to think or how to feel.

So she decides to act.

"Nakia?" she calls out as she climbs off the bed and looks for her shoes, hoping the guard can hear her through the thick door.

She can. Said door opens, and Nakia's head and armor-padded shoulders (*so* overkill) materialize in the room. "Yes, Your Majesty?"

Shuri spots her second shoe and grins in triumph. Then stands to pull both on. "Would you be so kind as to accompany me to my laboratory?"

The dodged message from Riri is brief: An eleven-year-old girl noted for her research on poisonous dart frog venom as a balm for chronic pain has disappeared from Ecuador.

Shuri holds her breath as she boots up the P.R.O.W.L. network to check for notifications . . . then exhales in a *whoosh* of relief when she sees that there are none.

Then, with K'Marah's resentment-laced voice ("*. . . you think all this disappearing-girls stuff is a silly waste of time . . .*") echoing in her head, Shuri adds the new name to the hit list—Pilar Bautista—and replies to Riri, letting the American girl know she's done so and "will let you know if there are any pings . . ."

But as she's typing the rest of her intended message— ". . . but there haven't been any on the other names, so don't get your hopes up"—a high-pitched sound rings out.

PING!

ALERT: KEYWORD *PILAR BAUTISTA*
LOCATION: PENDING . . .
TIME: 10:53
TRANSCRIPTION:
    ". . . BAUTISTA IS . . . [UNABLE TO TRANSCRIBE]. MAYBE IT'S ALL THE POISON SHE HANDLES."
    "OKAY . . ."

"I'M JUST SAYING, YOUR EXCELLENCY, WITH GIRLS LIKE *HER* AROUND, IT MIGHT BE WISE TO CONSIDER AN ALTERNATE MEANS OF KEEPING THE RECRUITS ... [UNABLE TO TRANSCRIBE]."

"GIRLS LIKE *HER* ... WHAT DOES THAT MEAN?"

"SHE APPEARS IMMUNE TO AUDITORY [UNABLE TO TRANSCRIBE]. AND IS GETTING SUSPICIOUS. SHE WAS OVERHEARD TALKING TO ANOTHER SPANISH-SPEAKING RECRUIT ABOUT 'SOMETHING' NOT BEING [UNABLE TO TRANSCRIBE]—"

LOCATION ACQUIRED: SOUTH TIGRAY, ETHIOPIA; 13.519, 39.423

SIGNAL LOST

END TRANSCRIPTION.

Shuri stares at those final two words on-screen, unable to breathe, let alone move or speak. Her eyes drift up a few lines to the pair of numbers, and her whole body locks up.

It's official: The princess has coordinates.

8

PRIORITIES

Except now, Shuri's not entirely sure of what to do. The coordinates place the ping just outside the Ethiopian city of Mekele at the western edge of the Danakil Depression. Which, as Shuri just learned forty-five seconds ago—is one of the lowest and driest places on Earth. It's also the hottest.

Other things she's learned? There are two active volcanoes, several salt plains—which many of the locals mine by hand with little more than a small ax—and multiple sulfur lakes with yellow-and-green mineral deposits that make the area look like an alien planet.

In fact, the more Shuri reads about this place, the more baffled she becomes. If Pilar Bautista was in fact kidnapped in Ecuador, why on earth would her captors take her to a bizarre desert landscape in Ethiopia?

She spends the next several hours scouring the interwebs for more information. Like the other "cases" (if one could even *call* them that), Pilar's disappearance is noted only in research chat groups and has yet to be reported to any authorities. What the princess *is* able to come up with: a photo of the girl wearing a medal that hangs to her navel at some international science fair that was held in Rio de Janeiro; an interview with an older man whose rheumatoid arthritis was relieved by the dart balm she created and was in the processes of patenting; and an obituary for the girl's mother. In the article attached to the medal photo, the girl says her mother's lupus-related aches and pains were the catalyst for her research.

The more Shuri reads, the more she realizes how *alike* she and this Ecuadorean girl are. Which, counter to what she thought would happen, read: giving her warm fuzzies that would spur her on to taking some valiant and potentially foolhardy action—only serves to make her more afraid. If the girl *is* being held somewhere within a pseudo-extraterrestrial landscape in middle-of-nowhere Ethiopia, fine . . . it's close by.

But also not fine at all. What is she supposed to do, hop into her *Predator* transport vessel and zip over to the coordinates? She has no idea what she'd be walking—or really *flying*—into.

"Your Majesty?" Nakia appears in the doorway to the lab station. "My apologies for the interruption, but it is near time for your scheduled assessment with Kocha M'Shindi."

That sure gets Shuri's attention. "My *what*, now?"

"Your assessment," Nakia repeats. "With the Kocha." She lifts her arm and taps a bead on her Kimoyo bracelet, and a purple-tinted schedule appears in midair. One line in the *Activity* column stands out in bold:

Quarter I Evaluation: Dambe and Nuba Fighting Moderator—Kocha M'Shindi

"Holy sh—"

"SHURI!"

"I was going to say *shamans*!" Shuri shouts, shutting down the P.R.O.W.L. network and shoving back from the desk to scramble to her feet. Of *all* the tests to forget! She scowls at the computer, furious. *When* had she blanked on this assessment? When Okoye asked her about K'Marah? When the message from Riri came in? She certainly hadn't been thinking about it this morning when K'Marah was in her quarters . . . *Bast*, this is bad!

"Are you all right, Your Majesty?" Nakia says, concern forming a canyon between her eyebrows.

"Fine, fine," Shuri says. She is maybe the furthest she's ever been from *fine*, but no need to tell Nakia that. There certainly isn't anything the Dora could do about Shuri's woes. Just as there is nothing Shuri can do about Pilar Bautista. Or any of the other girls for that matter.

All the princess can do in this particular moment is try and remember the differences between Dambe and Nuba. If she knows anything about the Kocha, it's that the old woman is likely to combine moves from both martial arts practices in a hand-to-hand combat contest, and then "assess" Shuri by making her say which strike/block/kick was from which discipline.

She tosses one last glance over her shoulder at the black of the powered-down computer monitor, and her reflection stares back at her.

Yes.

She'll do what she can: She'll nail this evaluation.

Shuri . . . doesn't. Nail the evaluation.

In fact, she doesn't even get the opportunity to *complete* the evaluation: When she and Nakia step into the

Kocha's training facility—a thatched hut out at the eastern edge of the baobab plain (though the woman *lives* in the penthouse of the sleekest building in Wakanda's capital)—M'Shindi takes one look at the princess, rolls her eyes, and turns away with a dismissive wave of her hand. "She is not ready," she says. "Bring her back when she has conquered her distraction."

And though Nakia spares Shuri the embarrassment of conversation en route back to the palace, what the Dora says once the hovercraft is parked in a palace-garage charging port is like salt in the Kocha stab wound: "Soooo . . . would you like to tell your mother, or should I?"

Shuri's head whips right. "Come again?"

"She is expecting a report of your results, Princess." The Dora meets Shuri's surely horrified gaze. "One of us will have to tell her you . . . weren't assessed. Unless you would prefer that the Kocha deliver the ne—"

"NO!"

This makes Nakia chuckle.

"Don't laugh at me, Nakia!" Shuri says, putting her face in her hands.

"My apologies, Your Majesty. It wasn't meant to be derisive."

Shuri sniffs. Not because she's *crying*, mind you. More because she's trying not to. Insult to injury, this whole shebang. The day began terribly, yet has some-how managed to get progressively worse.

"I hope you'll forgive what may be an imposition, Shuri, but ambitious woman to ambitious girl, you're a smidge hard on yourself. You are very near and dear to me, so understand that this is stated in love: The pursuits of your heart will neither hide nor flee from you. I know that this training regimen is important to you, but perhaps the source of your preoccupation in *this* moment should be given greater consideration."

Of all the things Shuri expected Nakia to say, this certainly wasn't one of them.

"Huh?"

"Well . . . I peeped in on you four times while we were at your laboratory. But you didn't notice. You were very much engrossed in whatever it is you were doing on your computer. I suspect from your shock at being reminded of today's assessment that your cyber activities were *not* related to your training?"

Shuri looks away. Which is enough of an answer.

"Perhaps more credence should be given to this *other* pursuit for now. It is clearly important enough to draw the whole of your attention."

Again, Shuri doesn't respond.

"You won't forsake your destiny by following your instincts, is all I'm saying. Give it some thought?"

Shuri's gaze falls to her hands. Her fingernails are bitten to nubs.

She sighs. And nods. "Okay," she says.

To Shuri's annoyance, the queen mother seemed *pleased* when Shuri mumbled the truth about what'd transpired at the Kocha's über-old-school training hut. "Hmmm," she'd practically purred, a twinkle dancing in her kohl-rimmed eyes. "Well, better luck next time, ey?"

The princess returned to her quarters with so much frustration swirling inside her, it's a wonder steam didn't shoot from all her facial orifices.

Now she's . . . pacing. Which is very much out of the ordinary. It's just . . . well, she has precisely zero sense of what to do. She could attempt to study, but that is likely to be an exercise in futility: "The capacity to retain information" is near the top of her *things I am presently lacking* list.

She could practice the martial arts moves she *didn't* get to exhibit today . . . but then she'd just hear M'Shindi's voice in her head, barking critiques of her form. (No, thank you.)

The telescope currently set up in her reading nook catches Shuri's eye. She's been using it to study celestial bodies—constellations, the rings of Saturn, a couple of different nebulae—for her Vibranium course, but in this moment, it reminds her of the missing girls. Didn't one of them discover a planetary system similar to the one Earth is a part of?

She stops pacing and sighs. Is Nakia right? *Should* she shift her focus to this . . . other matter? It's clearly not going to leave her alone. (Or perhaps it's *she* who can't leave *it* alone.)

But where to even begin?

Shuri returns to her pacing, hands clasped behind her back. She could start by telling Riri about the hit on Pilar's name. And the location. Maybe the region will spark something for Riri. Are any of the missing girls known for research that would make a mineral-rich—and funky-colored—salt flat valuable?

The other option, of course, is for Shuri to just *go* there. Maybe a quick flight, in stealth-mode obviously, to scope out the area from above. Do a few scans of the terrain—a topographic one, but an electromagnetic and maybe a thermodynamic as well.

She could probably talk Nakia into joining her under the guise of a study-related something or other . . . but then Shuri recalls her mother's seeming satisfaction at her lack of a training evaluation today. She wouldn't put it past the queen to shut down any request to leave the country even with a Dora Milaje in tow. *Especially* if the stated intentions are training-related.

A framed photograph on the small table beside Shuri's bed catches her eye. It's of Shuri and K'Marah kneeling in a field of glowing plants. Heart-shaped herb plants. The ones that have grown back since the girls' successful quest to rescue them.

Just the two of them.

But will K'Marah even *speak* to Shuri right now? Their last interaction wasn't exactly pleasant. If she calls, will K'Marah even ans—

There's a series of pounds on Shuri's door just before it flies open. "SHURI!" K'Marah shouts, rushing in like she's fleeing a chemical fire. She waves her Kimoyo card in the air. "Shuri, you will never believe it!"

"Believe what?" the princess says, so stunned to *see* K'Marah, she can't respond any other way.

"THIS," K'Marah says, shoving the smartphone-like device into Shuri's face. On the screen is a digital photo of what looks like an open greeting card. An exceedingly fancy cream-colored one with gilded edges. There are hieroglyphic-style symbols all around the margins, and the slightly blurred words are written in elaborate calligraphy. In French.

"It's an invitation," K'Marah says, just as Shuri parts her lips to ask what it is. "I just heard from Jojo—"

"From *whom*?"

"Josephine," K'Marah says. "My friend in France. She got caught sneaking out to pursue a lead on Celeste, so her parents confiscated her phone. That's why I hadn't heard from her."

"Ah." So K'Marah's panic *had* been unfounded. Shuri gulps down the impulse to point that out.

"Anyway, a few days ago, she received *that* in the mail. It's a . . . summons."

"Okay . . ." Shuri says. "To what?"

"That's the thing." She looks Shuri right in the eyes, worry coating her face like the wrong shade of makeup. "She wouldn't say. Do you remember how I told you she told *me* her cousin received an invitation she wouldn't tell *her* about?"

"Wait . . . who wouldn't tell whom—?"

"Doesn't matter. Point is, I think this might be the same thing."

Now Shuri's face scrunches. "Huh? Why would you think that?"

"Well, she said she was going away for a while, but she wanted to tell me so I wouldn't worry."

"Okay . . ."

"But *then* she goes, 'I'd rather not emulate my darling cousin and vanish without alerting my loved ones.'"

"Okay . . ."

"Which totally means she went to the same place,

doesn't it? She got her phone back and then went to *join* her cousin. Likely in the same place where all the other missing girls are being held!"

Shuri opens her mouth to respond, but then thinks better of it. Because in truth, the princess isn't entirely certain how to reply. Even *with* Shuri giving credence to the possibility that all the "disappearances" are interrelated, K'Marah's conclusion would be . . . a stretch (euphemistically speaking).

But how to express that without hurting her friend's feelings again?

"Uhh," Shuri begins. "Is there mention of an address on the invite?"

K'Marah rolls her eyes. "It's in *French*, remember? I have no idea!" She lifts the Kimoyo card to her face. "It looks like there may be some numbers here. Perhaps it's a street address?"

"Let me see," Shuri says, stalling to figure out how to bring her friend back to Earth.

Except what she sees on the screen snatches the air straight from her windpipe. Because those numbers? Shuri recognizes them. She spent a decent portion of the morning so distracted by them, the Kocha refused to evaluate her.

13.519, 39.423.

Coordinates. In the Danakil Depression.

MISSION LOG

I DO BELIEVE WE ARE IN OVER OUR HEADS.

Because I "have no chill," as K'Marah put it, she noticed my reaction to the numbers on the invitation. And I couldn't bring myself to lie to her . . . Actually, that is untrue. I, 100 percent, *would've* lied to her had I been able to come up with something viable quickly enough. And I wish I had.

Anyway, that's neither here nor there now. I told her everything. From the addition of Pilar Bautista's name, to the ping, to the bizarre location it revealed.

Of course K'Marah wanted to leave immediately.

It took some coaxing, but after a series of reminders about what happened the *last* time we snuck out of the country—"Yes, but this is *Ethiopia*, not London! It's much closer!" she said at first—she began to see sense. But she wouldn't relax completely (and leave so I could think) until there was a *Plan* with a *Timetable* and *Logistics.*

So thirty-six hours hence, she and I will be given a two-day reprieve from our respective training regimens to accompany Clothier Lwazi on a fabric hunt in Addis Ababa. And since everyone is convinced the trip will be "good" for us, we are being permitted to travel with no Dora guard in tow. (Which might be due to Mother's not wanting to offend the clothier by suggesting that he is unable to handle K'Marah and me. Either way: works for us!)

We convinced him to ask Mother if we could all go in the *Predator* since it is both the fastest *and* safest travel vessel in the nation. Which will hopefully permit us to zip over to the Danakil Depression to scan the terrain for heat signatures, and then get back before he can get *too* angry about us disappearing. The flight between the two points shouldn't take more than one-half hour each way.

At least that's what I told K'Marah. In truth, there are infinite ways the whole shebang could go terribly wrong. Because one thing we *didn't* really discuss/plan is precisely what we intend to do once we get there.

I hate to even consider the possibility (I've avoided doing just that up to this point), but what happens if all the missing girls *are* there somewhere? And . . . we find them? What will come next? I certainly don't have the space or time to pile everyone into the *Predator* and deliver them to their respective homes around the world . . .

The fact that neither K'Marah nor I had the courage to bring this up during our discussion feels more ominous than I care to admit. Because surely she was thinking about it, too? I have yet to tell Riri about our plan . . . What would I even say?

There is no turning back now, though, I suppose. Perhaps since this is a goodwill mission, Bast/the gods/the universe/luck/whatever-entity-determines-the-outcome-of-these-sorts-of-unpredictable-things will work in our favor, and nothing will go too terribly wrong . . .

Here goes nothing, I guess.

9
DINE AND DITCH

verything goes terribly wrong.

First, Shuri oversleeps on the morning of the scheduled jaunt. Which is very much *un*like her, but she'd tossed and turned for most of the night before, plagued by terrible dreams that left her sweat-soaked and hopelessly tangled in her sheets.

Second, what finally *does* manage to break through to her unconscious mind—after six missed alarms—is a blaring signal from her Kimoyo card. In a haze, she grabs it from the small table beside her bed and manages to swipe in the right direction. As the words on the screen begin to swim into focus, she taps a spot near the bottom that seems important (she thinks it says *listen*?) . . . And then two voices fill the air and snatch her awake so fast, she literally gasps:

". . . glad she is taking this breather. This trip with Clothier Lwazi and break from all that combat *stuff is the best thing for her right now, I think."*

"I have zero doubt you think that, Mother. In fact, I am certain the entire palace knows how you really *feel about Shuri's training."*

<long pause>

"I have no idea what you mean, T'Challa."

"Uh-huh. Whatever you say, My Queen."

"Think what you will. I just feel that this training thing is distracting our girl from what really matters."

"And that would be . . . what, exactly?"

"Well . . . her studies, for one."

<long pause>

"What is that look, T'Challa? You disagree?"

"I mean you no disrespect, Mother, but Shuri is very much excelling in her studies. Even the additional ones she has taken on as part of her training regimen."

(At this, Shuri exhales. Maybe her big-headed brother isn't so bad after all.)

"For now she is excelling. But we both know how these things go. Even M'Shindi has expressed some concerns about Shuri's waver-ing focus. Thank Bast the woman had the presence of mind to turn her away the other day! Who knows what sort of damage she may have done handling weapons—"

"There are no weapons in Dambe or Nuba, Umama."

"Wellll . . . either way. I am telling you, T'Challa: That child is not ready for all this. Just yesterday I passed by her near the kitchens, and she didn't even notice me, she was so lost in thought. The bags beneath her eyes are beginning to rival those of the River Eldress. I don't want to stifle her ambitions, but I'm not sure it's wise for her to accompany you to this conclave. Even if she were to pull through on the assessments—"

"Shuri?"

The door begins to open, and quick as she can, Shuri silences the transmission and shoves the Kimoyo card beneath her pillow.

Nakia peeks in. "Ah, you're awake now. My apologies for the intrusion . . . Just thought I heard voices that weren't yours . . ." Her eyes narrow.

Shuri clears her throat. "Nope! Just me! I can be a bit . . . *froggy* some mornings."

"Ah. Talking to yourself."

"Do you, umm . . . know what time it is?" Shuri tosses in a deeply unconvincing yawn and rub of the eyes to sell her supposed bleariness.

Nakia nods. "The time is nine forty-two, Your Highness."

"NINE FORTY-TWO?!" Shuri is out of bed and into her closet faster than she can process how she got there. "OH MY GODS!"

By the time she comes back out—approximately thirty-seven seconds later—Nakia is fully inside the room.

"Are you all right, Shuri?"

No. She is not all right. "I'm fine!" Where is K'Marah? Why didn't she wake Shuri up? There's no way *she* overslept . . .

"You didn't happen to see K'Marah anywhere this morning, did you?"

"Oh yes! She came by a few times."

Shuri freezes in the midst of pulling on a sock. "She did?"

"Yes. I told her you were sleeping. She was none

too thrilled when I sent her away for good after her third try—I told her *you* would contact *her* when you woke. But she'll be fine. I know the two of you have plans today, but you needed your rest."

Shuri sure hopes *she* will be fine once she does contact her best friend. K'Marah will certainly be in a *mood* considering how behind schedule they are.

The princess slips her shoes on, fishes her Kimoyo card from its hiding place (Nakia's brow lifts at this), and shoves it into the cargo pocket of her favorite pants before grabbing her knapsack and rushing to the door. "Well, thanks for looking out for me!" she says to the Dora as she approaches.

"Ahh, Princess?" Nakia steps into Shuri's path, her hands clasped in front of her.

She doesn't have time for this! The princess stops and forces a smile. "Yes?"

"You're, umm . . . missing a shirt."

Shuri looks down. There's her purple sports bra . . . and then her bare midriff. "Oh," she says. "Right." She spins on her heel and heads back to the closet. Fully aware from the feeling in her gut that things will only get worse from here.

And worse they do get. While the Dora-in-training doesn't *seem* as upset as Shuri expects her to be, when

K'Marah's dear uncle, darling clothier of Shuri's mother, sees the *Predator*, he outright refuses to travel within it. It takes K'Marah committing to cleaning his workshop from top to bottom, Shuri promising him an additional week of paid vacation time (her mother will certainly "ground" her for that one), and both girls asking him to make the gowns for when they graduate from their respective training programs—"You can choose *those* fabrics today as well!"—to get him to budge.

By then, they're an additional twenty-eight minutes behind.

The flight to Ethiopia is relatively smooth, barring one particularly powerful pocket of turbulence during which the clothier has to lie down. Not that Shuri would *tell* the others, but the only reason the *Predator* gets caught in the shifting winds is because she zones out thinking about the overheard conversation between T'Challa and her mother, and she fails to climb the vessel to a higher altitude in time to dodge the rough air.

Once they're on the ground, though—three hours and seventeen minutes later than anticipated, and after having to park on top of a two-story building in stealth-mode post letting K'Marah and Lwazi out on the ground—the girls quickly discover that getting *away* from Lwazi will be more difficult than they anticipated.

He's ... more *skittish* than Shuri would've imagined. Wants both girls by his side at all times. Not out of some instinctive urge to keep *them* safe, but because *he* is wildly uncomfortable in this new place.

Which, to Shuri, is baffling. As her head swivels to take in their surroundings—they're in a place called Merkato, where merchants of all sorts have their wares on display for purchase—she can't help but beam. At the brightly colored garments and head wraps, the petrol-powered vehicles, and the hustle-bustle of the place. There are laughing children, and people on bicycles, and varying shades of beautiful brown skin, and the air smells of coffee, herbs, and spices: cinnamon and rosemary and black pepper. Shuri's heart swells when one shopkeeper shouts across the way to another one in Amharic. *Good day*, she makes out from her brief encounter with the language in East African studies during primary school.

Clothier Lwazi just about jumps out of his skin. The three of them are leaving a "deeply disappointing," as he put it, fabric kiosk, and Lwazi grabs both K'Marah's and Shuri's upper arms more tightly than either girl feels is strictly necessary.

Shuri and K'Marah exchange a look. "Uncle, you've

been outside Wakanda before, yes?" K'Marah asks.

"Of course, of course," he replies, peeking around as though some known assassin is lurking nearby, out to get them all.

"But never to *this* city, I presume?" Shuri says upon being pulled into a vaguely absurd (speed) walking pace.

"Oh, I've certainly been to this city," he replies. "I *love* this city. Once found the most gorgeous printed linen I've ever laid eyes on." He kicks a furtive glance over his shoulder.

"So why do you seem so nervous?" Thank Bast for K'Marah. Gets right to the point, that one does.

"I'm not really into *crowds*," he says. "Ooh, come on! I see another fabric stand just ahead!"

They continue on like this—Lwazi clinging to them like that elastane fabric Shuri used to make T'Challa's latest Panther Habit, while zipping around in abject terror—for the most excruciating seventy-three minutes of Shuri's young life. Lwazi has collected multiple reams of myriad fabrics, but Shuri and K'Marah have accomplished little more than being promoted from fabric-shopping mascots to textile-stuffed-bag carriers.

When Lwazi begins the bartering process with yet another merchant, K'Marah gets as close as she can to

Shuri (the young Dora's uncle is still between them, holding one of each of their hands as if they're five-year-olds). "We need an intervention," she whispers to the princess.

"Oh, you think?"

"Sarcasm doesn't suit you, Princess. Got any ideas?"

"He's *your* uncle! What do *you* think we should do?"

"If I knew, I would've done it alrea—"

"Ladies, I'm *famished*," Lwazi cuts in, wholly oblivious to their scheming. "What do you say we snatch a bite to eat and then head home? I've certainly found more options than I expressly needed. Don't mention that to your mother, Miss Shuri."

"Oh, I would never!" Shuri replies. She looks back at K'Marah, who rolls her eyes in her uncle's direction . . . but then her brows rise, and her face lights up brighter than Wakanda's capital on T'Challa's birthday.

"I know where we should eat!" she shouts. More enthusiastically than Shuri feels is warranted considering the circumstances.

"Oh, you do?" Lwazi says. "And how would you know that?"

"I sought out some food options last night in case we got hungry. Didn't know how long we'd be here."

She tugs her hand from Lwazi's grip and removes her Kimoyo card from her pocket. Taps for a second and then: "Come on. It's this way."

Shuri and the clothier can do nothing but follow. Though the princess does manage to free up her hand as well.

K'Marah's bizarre behavior continues once they are all seated. She orders the same dish as her uncle, though he asks for his without butter, then proceeds to doodle on a paper napkin with a pen she borrowed from the server until the food comes. And then once it's on the table, she (over)excitedly points out a pregnant woman in a beautiful wrap-style sundress with matching head scarf. Shuri and Lwazi both turn to look. It *is* a lovely outfit. ("Oh my! I wonder where I could find *that* fabric!" Lwazi says.)

But then five minutes into the meal, Lwazi sits up, straight as a pin. "Oh no," he says.

"Uncle? Are you all right?"

He turns his body to her without moving his head. "They definitely cooked my meal in butter. If you ladies will excuse me—" And he stands and waddles in the direction of what Shuri guesses is the bathroom.

"Whoa—"

"Let's go," K'Marah says, jumping up from her seat. She takes the napkin with her doodles—and words, Shuri can now see—and places it beside the clothier's plate. "We'll even take the bags so he won't have to."

"*Go?*" from Shuri. "Go *where*?"

"To those coordinates!" K'Marah practically shouts. "We need to move *now*. There's no telling how quickly he may come back."

It clicks. "K'Marah, did you switch your uncle's plate to the one with butter?"

"Hmm? Oh, that reminds me!" And she switches them back. "He'll be fine, I promise," she says with a wave. "Lactose *low*-tolerant. Just a little gas, I'm sure. Now, come on! We have some girls to save!"

And with a forlorn look at her uneaten *doro wat*, Shuri stands and takes off behind her friend.

10

CLOAKED

The girls have just begun their ascent when K'Marah's Kimoyo card *and* bracelet ring out not quite simultaneously. Like a cacophony of *Hey, you two are going to be grounded forever* alarms.

"It's Uncle," she says, looking at the card screen. (Duh.) "And . . . Okoye."

Oh gods. "We are in *so* much trouble."

"The Okoye call might be nothing." K'Marah slides her bracelet from her wrist and stretches it out to the princess.

Who looks at it like it will make all of her fingers fall off. "What are you giving it to *me* for?"

"To answer, obviously! I need to take this call from Uncle! Here." And she tosses it at Shuri, who catches it with one hand to keep from being thwacked in the forehead with it. "Nice hands!" K'Marah adds with a wink as she leaps from her copilot seat and bolts toward the back of the *Predator*.

Within Shuri's fist, the ringing piece of jewelry continues to vibrate, a purple glow pulsing from somewhere deep within. It's *dramatic*, she knows, but in this moment, it almost feels like holding the fate of everything she knows in the palm of her hand.

The first time she opened a Kimoyo bead, she was six years old, and she's been instrumental in updating the technology. So she knows to turn off the *Predator*'s GPS signal before answering the call. She keeps the untraceable one on her Kimoyo card going so she can manually keep the vessel on course, but still: Cutting their sole way of being tracked means the lies she's about to tell the general are premeditated. The whole thing makes Shuri feel as if her insides are coated in that mutated toxin K'Marah's former flame, Henbane, used to decimate Wakanda's heart-shaped herb supply. (The princess's best friend sure knows how to pick 'em . . .)

She swallows back the sick feeling, and taps the bead to answer.

"Ahh . . . Hi, Okoye!" The general's upper half blooms from the bead in hologram form. (Shuri, of course, is *not* projecting back. She is also thankful for the *audio only* feature she added a few years back at T'Challa's request. He snuck out way more often than she could in a lifetime.)

Okoye's majestic features smush together as her head drops to one side. "Shuri? Is that you?"

"Yep!"

"Huh." She looks down at her own braceleted arm. "I could swear I called K'Marah . . ."

"You did!" Shuri says. Way too cheerfully. She clears her throat and tries to tone it down: "My apologies for the confusion, General. K'Marah is . . ." Shuri peeks over her shoulder, where she can barely make out K'Marah's muffled voice through the lavatory door. Hopefully, if Okoye can hear it, she'll chalk it up to Addis Ababa background noise. "She's in the restroom."

"Ah," Okoye says. "Strange that she would remove her communication beads for such a thing, but I won't play at comprehending you young people and your ways. Whereabouts are you all? I can't seem to locate a signal."

"Oh, umm . . . Still very much in Ethiopia! The clothier is *very* picky about fabric—"

"WOW, that was a close one!" K'Marah practically hollers as she steps out of the small washroom. Shuri makes a slicing motion at her throat and nods toward Okoye's floating half form. The shorter girl claps both hands over her mouth, but it's too late.

"K'Marah? Is that you?" the general says. "Will you two project so I can speak to your faces, please?"

"Ahh, sorry, General Okoye!" K'Marah shouts, grabbing a sheet of tissue paper from around one of the fabric bolts. "The service here isn't great!" She crumples the thin paper so it makes a loud crackling sound. "We'll have to call you back!"

Okoye lifts a cupped hand to her ear. "What was that? I can't really hear you—"

"Precisely!" K'Marah says, rustling the paper more fervently.

Now Okoye's eyes narrow. "This better not be some sort of trick, K'Marah. We need to discuss your most recent failed evaluation—"

"You're breaking up!" K'Marah shouts. Then she makes a gods-awful noise in the back of her throat. "We're losing you—"

She ends the call.

"WHEW," she says, dropping back down into the

seat beside Shuri. "All bullets dodged. I told Uncle we needed to go scan some terrain for science class and wanted to spare him the additional time in the air."

Shuri's eyebrows rise. "And he bought that?"

"Oh, surely not," K'Marah says. "But I'm sure he's appreciating the time *alone* to shop. He did confess that much of his anxiety was rooted in having to keep an eye on *us*. Never been one for babysitting, Uncle," she goes on. "I told him we'd return for him in a couple of hours. Hopefully that's enough time for us to complete the mission."

The princess is fighting hard to regain what little chill she typically possesses, so she keeps her eyes straight ahead.

"How much longer until we get there?" K'Marah says, tapping at the navigation screen. "Wait, why isn't it working?"

After a long and exceedingly deep breath, Shuri turns to her friend. "We need to go back," she says.

"What? No way," comes K'Marah's response. "Those girls *need* our help and we're, what, fifteen minutes from giving it to them?"

"How exactly are we going to help them, K'Marah?" Shuri surprises even herself with the calmness of her voice. Because inside? She's screaming. This is an infinitely bigger deal than either Shuri or her almost–Dora

Milaje best friend are prepared to handle. Yes: She is princess of a sovereign nation with access to more resources than she's sure any of the potentially missing girls have ever seen. But last she checked, Wakanda isn't in the habit of involving itself in matters that . . . are not pertinent to the continued safety and prosperity of Wakanda.

And for good reason, as far as the princess is concerned: Enemies, known and unknown, are everywhere. If there's one thing Shuri *has* retained from Scholar M'Walimu's courses, it's the understanding that if your nation has something another nation feels *they* should have, the latter will stop at nothing to acquire what they're after. As far as Shuri is concerned, "war" could be an acronym for "Wanting Another's Resources."

Even with all that aside, there's no one here but *them* right now. A relatively powerless princess of an unknown nation, and a royal guard . . . who hasn't even completed her training. How much *help* could the pair of girls really be?

"What do you mean?" But Shuri can hear the waver in K'Marah's voice. This *has* crossed the Dora trainee's mind.

"You know exactly what I mean. Even if the girls *are* at this mystery location—which I highly doubt, considering the images I've seen of it—what exactly are you . . . well, *we*, planning to do to 'help' them?"

"Well . . ." When Shuri peeks over, K'Marah is fidgeting with the hem of her (ridiculous coral-beaded) tunic. "I mean. We can alert the authorities—"

"*What* authorities? These girls' parents didn't alert any authorities. We could tell my mom and brother, obviously—which *then* involves my sharing where I got the information and being grounded quite possibly forever—but there are too many unknown variables here, K'Marah." Shuri stops there, but her thoughts are swirling. What if—Bast forbid—the girls' guardians got rid of them on purpose? Or . . . sold them off? Shuri came across a number of horrifying stories while investigating this whole deal with Riri. This is all so far above the princess's pay grade.

K'Marah huffs, straightens her back, and lifts her chin. "We'll have to at least *try*, Shuri. Especially if no one else is!"

At this, Shuri breaks. "This is a . . . wild-duck hunt—"

"Goose chase," K'Marah says.

"What?!"

"The expression is *wild-goose chase*. And you can't know that, Shuri. Those girls could be in serious danger! What kind of people would *we* be if we don't check out this lead?"

"But it might not even *be* a lead! We're running off and telling lies and potentially ruining everything we've worked for, and for what?"

"Oh, come on, Shuri. You're like a wizard of Vibranium and a master inventor. You're the smartest person I know. There is no way on earth *or* the ancestral plane that you would be here if you truly believed this to be a wild-goose chase."

Shuri has nothing to say to that.

"I know you're scared." K'Marah's hand lands on Shuri's arm. "I am, too. And fine: I *don't* know what we'll do if we find something at those coordinates. But you and I both know we have to at least look. If we don't, it'll eat away at us for . . . our entire eternity in the Djalia!"

Shuri takes a deep breath and turns the *Predator*'s GPS back on. And within four minutes, a disembodied voice fills the air: "*You are arriving at your destination.*"

All of Shuri's high-tech tools are useless: The combination of high heat, sulfur-poisoned air, and complete lack of atmospheric moisture make the landscape virtually unscannable. Which means they'll have to land.

("Can't have come this far for nothing, right?" K'Marah says, coaxing when the princess wavers. "If we're going to get grounded, we might as well make it worthwhile.")

The closest city—Mekele—is approximately 112 kilometers due west, so hopefully there won't be any emergencies. Where K'Marah was lying about spotty service when talking to Okoye fifteen minutes ago, she'd certainly be telling the truth now.

Shuri puts the *Predator* down one hundred meters or so south of their coordinate spot. Then she goes to the small closet on board. "Here," she says to K'Marah, tossing her what looks like a rolled-up purple trash bag. "Vibranium-enhanced polyethylene coveralls. *With* an Invisi-mode. And once you zip in and exhale, the carbon dioxide in your breath will activate the oxygenation system built into the hood. The mask part is made from a special polymer I created, so we'll be completely protected without any obstruction to our vision." With a snap, the princess unfurls a matching jumpsuit for herself.

"You have hazmat suits just sitting in your hovercraft's closet?" K'Marah asks. "Actually, don't answer that. Because of course you do."

Shuri shrugs. "You never know when you'll need one."

Once they're off the *Predator*—which Shuri leaves in Invisi-mode—the girls . . . have no idea what to do next.

K'Marah speaks first: "Where is the *exact* spot?"

"Right over there." Shuri points, holding her Kimoyo card over her head to get a signal.

"Mmmmm . . ."

Shuri looks at the spot.

There's nothing there.

But then—

She gasps. "Did you see that?"

"See what?" K'Marah asks, looking around. "All I see is . . . alien paradise."

"There was a flash just ahead," Shuri replies. "At least I think there was."

"Okaaaay . . . So now what?"

Under any other circumstances, Shuri would assume her eyes had played a trick on her—especially in a deeply unforgiving terrain like this one.

But she has a *feeling*. Not that she'd say such a thing to K'Marah. "Let's get closer to the exact spot, and then we can go."

"Uhh, okay."

So they walk. And the farther they go, the more the air in front of them seems to . . . bend.

"Huh," K'Marah says.

There's a *ping!* and a choppy, garbled sound issues from the device in Shuri's hand. *You ha—each—you—estin—a—on.*

A seed of dread buries itself in the center of the princess's chest, and the roots spread: out to her arms and down into her belly and legs.

In front of them is . . . nothing. Hot, salt-flat land-scape as far as the eye can see.

And yet—

"I think I'm having déjà vu," K'Marah says, slowly stretching her hand forward.

"K'Marah, wait!"

But the other girl's hand stops dead in midair. Against something solid.

There's a flicker in front of Shuri, and her head whips back just in time to catch a brief glimpse of her own reflection.

"Shuri, this is like your—"

"*Predator*'s Invisi-mode mechanism," the princess breathes as the shock of it all trickles down over her.

"But *how*?" K'Marah breathes. "Didn't you *invent* that?"

Shuri gulps and doesn't respond. She guesses it's possible someone else in the world was able to devise a similar tech. But she can't shake the feeling that this is *her* design. The implications of which are staggering.

Because the only entity in the world that *should* have access to her cloaking schematic is the American counter-terrorism organization she hacked when designing the *Predator.* She'd left the Invisi-mode details as a form of payment for the blueprints she borrowed.

Strategic Homeland Intervention, Enforcement, and Logistics Division: S.H.I.E.L.D.

If S.H.I.E.L.D. is involved in this missing-girls thing . . .

They need to leave. Immediately.

"K'Marah, we have to go!" Shuri says, taking a step back as her pulse begins to race. She shakes her head in an attempt to clear it. They'll return to Wakanda, and she will tell T'Challa everything. Even if she gets into trouble, it's the right thing to do. Let the adults handle this one. She looks around for her friend, whom she swears was beside her just a second ago. "K'Marah, where are—"

"SHURI!" K'Marah shouts, suddenly running in Shuri's direction.

The princess has never been so relieved. "There you are," she says. "Listen, I really think we should le—"

"You have to come!" K'Marah grabs Shuri's arms and tries to pull her forward.

"K'Marah! You're not listening! We are in *danger*—"

"No, *you're* not listening!" K'Marah says, whipping back around to face the princess. Shuri is shocked by the *elation* she can see on her friend's face through the clear mask of her suit.

"Shuri," K'Marah says, jubilant. "You won't believe it! I found the door!"

11

(SORT OF) BREAKING
AND ENTERING

We have to go invisible," Shuri says before taking a single step. She knows there's no way they'll be leaving this incongruously briny desert wasteland without going into whatever *thing* is hidden here in plain sight. K'Marah would pitch an entire fit.

And fine: Shuri is also curious (though terrified).

"What?" comes K'Marah's reply.

"We have to go invisible before we go in there. We

should probably be invisible *now*. Whatever this thing is, there could be cameras."

"Oh . . . Maybe should've thought of that sooner?"

"I wasn't expecting to actually *find* anything!" the princess barks.

"Okay, fine. So how do we go invisible?"

"At the base of your left palm, where hand meets wrist, there's a button built into the suit. Don't press it yet because when you do, I won't be able to see you—"

"Isn't that the entire *point*?" K'Marah snaps.

"Look, being snippy isn't going to get us anywhere," the princess says. "While it's great that you found a door, do not neglect to consider that we have precisely zero idea of what we are walking into. We don't know why this—whatever it is—is *here*, hidden from view in one of the world's most inhospitable places. We don't know who put it here or what's inside it. So we'd do well to proceed with caution instead of charging ahead like a pair of rhinoceroses in a pottery shop—"

"Okay, okay!" K'Marah raises both hands in surrender. "Point taken!"

Shuri nods, satisfied. For the moment at least. "Turn in the direction we need to walk to get to the door, and I'll put my right hand on your right shoulder before we push our buttons."

"Okay." K'Marah rotates 180 degrees so that her

back is to the princess, and Shuri claps a hand on her shoulder.

"Ready? One . . . two . . ."

"WAIT!" K'Marah peeks back, wide-eyed. "You did *test* this Invisi-suit thingy, right? It's not going to malfunction and make us permanently unseeable?"

"*Three*," Shuri says through gritted teeth. And then her hand vanishes a beat before the shoulder it's sitting on disappears.

"WHOA," K'Marah's formless voice says both out of *and* into what very much looks like the proverbial void. "This is . . . I mean, it's like literally *nothing*. Yes, I can see the inside of my hood or whatever in my peripheral vision, but I *feel* your hand on my shoulder and my hand on the invisible kidnapper's prison—"

"Oh my gods. Can we just go to the door?"

"I'm going, I'm going. It's difficult to walk when you can't see your feet *or* the thing you're walking alongside!"

Shuri considers this . . . as well as how difficult it is to walk *behind* someone she can't actually see. "Fair," she says.

"I'm going to keep talking because if I don't, I might start freaking out. This is . . . a lot. This invisibility while in pursuit of something invisible."

"Also fair. How much farther?"

"It's just ahead. I put a large hunk of oddly colored salt—that's what most of this is, yes?—right in front of it."

"Ah. Okay."

"You'll be proud of me," K'Marah continues. "You'd totally zoned out, so I decided to explore a bit. I just kept my hand along the side of this thing, and eventually, there was ... an *anomaly*, as you would put it. Like a break in the super-smooth line. Honestly, if not for all the precision exercises we have to do in Dora training, I doubt I would've felt it. So I guess that's something. Anyway, I decided to follow the anomaly with my fingertips—*within* the suit, of course. I'm no idiot. And that's when I discovered that it went straight up, hit a right angle, then straight across before hitting another right angle and heading back down. Voilà. A door. Here we are."

K'Marah turns abruptly, and Shuri crashes into her, then stumbles right, tripping over a jagged crystal-looking thing the size of a soccer ball. Not that she's ever seen snow in person, but K'Marah's salt hunk marker looks like the type American films tell children not to eat: It's yellow. "Ow," the princess says.

"Sorry."

Shuri stands and dusts off—though there's no reason to. The cloaking tech is designed to camouflage anything that sits on the suit for longer than three milli-seconds. Which is how she knows that even if she were to toss a full bucket of paint at the space where K'Marah says the door is, it wouldn't help them see it. "So . . . how do we get in?" she says to (perceivably) no one.

"Right," K'Marah's voice replies. "That's the part I haven't quite figured out yet."

Shuri smacks her forehead. "K'Marah!"

"What? I got us this far! You're the supposed genius he—"

"Please confirm the password," comes a disembodied voice out of quite literally nowhere.

Shuri, also quite literally, jumps. "Ummm—"

"That is incorrect. Please confirm the password."

"This is bad—" K'Marah begins, but is swiftly cut off. Because the voice speaks out again: "That is incorrect. Warning: You have one final attempt. An incorrect password will result in an intruder alert."

Neither girl says a word. Shuri can't *breathe*, let alone speak.

She knows the same is true for K'Marah when she feels the other girl's hand close around her wrist and squeeeeeeze—

"Please confirm the password."

Shuri gulps. In spite of the cooling mechanism built

into the suit, she can feel the sweat beading at her hair-
line and rolling down her sides from beneath her arms.
They have one shot to either crack this or tuck tail
and run—which will be impossible without making
themselves visible, and if there *are* cameras, they're
surely trained on the two girls now. Totally fine as long
as there's nothing to see . . . But if they *do* have to reveal
themselves? The princess doesn't even want to think
about the trouble that might be awaiting them.

If they manage to make it inside, though, Shuri figures it's possible to hide until whatever security entity
involved does a sweep and decides the whole incident
was some sort of glitch.

But they have to actually get *in*—

"Please confirm the password."

Okay. Shuri can figure this out . . .

"Twelve seconds to intruder alert."

K'Marah's grip on Shuri's arm tightens to the point
where the princess almost cries out, but she clenches
her jaw and swallows it down. She'll punch the Dora-
in-training when—if?—they make it out of this.

". . . nine . . . eight . . ."

Think, Shuri!

The voice definitely *responded* to something
K'Marah was saying. When exactly had she been cut
off? Could the password be one of the words she'd

just spoken? The voice *is* saying "confirm." Is this a stretch?

". . . five . . . four . . ."

Stretch or not, Shuri has to say *something*. Fast. The alarm will go off even if they stay silent, so it's too late to run. Might as well try?

THINK, Shuri!

"*I got us this far . . .*" K'Marah had said. "*You're the*—"

"Two . . . one . . ."

"GENIUS?" Shuri shouts before wrenching away from K'Marah and whipping around to cover her ears and brace herself before the alarm sounds. She guesses if she gets captured, she can't get grounded? Though knowing her mother, she and K'Marah will be found somehow and will be grounded *after* they're rescued. If the rescuers get here in time, at least.

How on earth did Shuri wind up here? She *knew* this was certain to go badly and yet—

"Access granted."

There's a sliding sound behind her and then: "You did it, Shuri!" in an ecstatic whisper. "Come on!"

The next minutes are a blur. Shuri doesn't fully remember rotating and crossing the threshold into the dark rectangular space that has appeared in front of them like some portal to another dimension, but she *does* know that the door they couldn't see from the outside glides home, and seals them in with a *whoosh* and a *click*.

There's no one manning the entrance. Which suggests that whoever is occupying this space is either exceedingly confident that no person who isn't supposed to be here could get in, or is *over*confident, and therefore exceedingly stupid. Perhaps both?

K'Marah finds Shuri's hand again, and the Wakandan girls interlace their fingers and hold tight. While Shuri can't see what K'Marah is up to, the princess hopes her friend is presently doing what she is: taking in their surroundings.

There's not a whole lot to see, though the entry hall is much taller than Shuri would've expected. Now that her eyes have adjusted from the brightness outside, she can see that the space is a perfect hexagon, illuminated by a line of continuous light—likely LED—that rings the room near the ceiling. The walls are bare, but painted to look like mahogany wood. Even from a distance Shuri knows it's not *real* wood because . . . well, she doesn't know *how* she knows. But she does. Right at Shuri's eye level, there's a multi-line design carved all the way around the otherwise empty interior: a double helix.

What she doesn't see is an exit. Either back out into

the hostile salt flat they just escaped, or farther into the mysterious edifice. There has to be *more* to this place, doesn't there? Why would someone hide an empty building in an uninhabitable desert region of Ethiopia—

"Welcome to the Garden."

Shuri and K'Marah both jump—and squeak—as the same disembodied voice from outside comes at them from all directions.

"Is that why it smells like spicy flowers in here?" K'Marah says.

Which is when Shuri notices the smell as well, though faintly. Wherever *here* is, there's enough oxygen in the air for that part of their suits to shut off.

"We thank you for accepting our invitation and are delighted to have you with us. Please proceed to the elevator."

A gap appears in the smooth wall directly in front of the girls. Beyond it? A smaller hexagonal space with floor-to-ceiling mirrors.

"How do they manage to hide all the doors?" K'Marah whispers.

"Shh!" Shuri replies.

"I'm just saying! That wall looked solid as stone! And speaking of looking, how weird is it to look into a mirror and see nothing—"

"You have to stop talking so you don't get us caught!" Though it does cross the princess's mind that they may already be caught. They're invisible, yes, but can the system *sense* their presence?

"Hmph," grunts K'Marah.

Shuri tugs K'Marah forward. And she does have to *tug*: It seems that despite the Dora-in-training's insistence on this entire mission, their lack of reflections in the elevator's glass walls has finally shaken her. (You know, since the whole invisible-building-in-a-salt-flat-wasteland thing didn't.)

The single-panel door slides home, and Shuri's heart makes a rapid ascent into her throat. Not because they've begun to move—at least she doesn't *think* they have—but because K'Marah is right: Standing in a mirrored box and seeing nothing is . . . uncomfortable.

"Perhaps this wasn't a good idea—"

"*Shhhhh!*" comes K'Marah's mocking retort.

Shuri opens her mouth to respond, but the words stick in her chest: A panel identical to the one that shut them in opens behind them, and the mirror that's missing *their* reflection gives view to a flurry of girls moving through a hallway in different-colored, long-sleeved jumpsuits. Voices and music whirl into the now-open elevator. (*When had they* moved??)

And then the voices fade to nothing as the brightly lab-suited lasses begin to take notice of the open elevator door.

"What the . . . ?" one in blue says, stopping midstride. Shuri could swear she and the girl—about her age, with thick blond hair in a braid draped over her shoulder—are staring right into each other's eyes.

Shuri can't breathe.

Especially when a small crowd gathers around the blue-outfitted girl. A ridiculous thought arises in the princess's mind as she looks at the multihued clump of young ladies: It's like she and K'Marah have been caught by a gang of human hard candies.

"Is there supposed to be a new arrival today?" comes the voice of a girl in yellow. She has beige-ish skin and wavy sandy-brown hair.

"I think Lady N would've told us about it . . ." blue replies.

"Also," says a medium-brown-skinned, short-haired girl in red, "there's nobody in there?" She pushes her glasses up on her nose.

Shuri isn't sure she's *ever* felt so relieved—though it doesn't last long. Because there's no ignoring the fact that it appears K'Marah was onto something: While none of the girls *they're* looking for are in the small crowd behind them, it's hard to deny the . . .

similarities between the ones they can see. All are female-presenting and appear to be around the same age as the Wakandan princess and her Dora-Milaje-in-training best friend.

Shuri's got a hunch they're all wicked smart, too.

"You have arrived. Please step out of the elevator."

(Shuri is really beginning to hate that automated voice.)

"There's gotta be a glitch or something," an East Asian girl in green says with a wave of her hand. "Probably fine for now. There's clearly no one there, so—"

"What if someone got the coordinates?" pipes up a tiny, timid-looking brunette in pink. She appears a bit younger than the others. Likely no more than nine or ten. Her hair is pulled up high in a tight bun, and Shuri wonders how a person so small could look so . . . serious.

"Syd, the elevator is literally empty, babe," says girl in yellow.

"Please step out of the elevator," the voice repeats.

"Definitely a glitch," from red.

"But what if they're just like . . . invisible or something?"

Now Shuri is the one squeezing the life out of K'Marah's hand. Though she doesn't dare move. Yes, the suits have a Vibranium-based coating and any motion *should* be soundless, but in this moment, the princess isn't sure about much of anything.

"Please step out of the elevator."

The brunette's eyes narrow—Syd, Shuri thinks she heard the girl called—and she takes a step toward the elevator. Shuri is fairly certain her heart is no longer beating.

But then girl in blue grabs Syd's arm and pulls her back. "Let's maybe *not* go near the demon elevator, kiddo. How about you head down to the main office and let Lady N know it opened on its own and is being weird."

Now Shuri *does* move: She rotates her body toward K'Marah's and reaches for the Dora-in-training's opposite hand so she can turn them both around.

Just in time, too.

"The elevator will now return you to the main entrance," the voice says. And the panel begins to slide shut.

Before she can think too much about it, Shuri steps forward and slides her foot across the threshold, hoping this elevator works the same way most others do.

She sends a silent prayer of thanks to Bast when the door flies back open.

"There is an obstruction blocking the elevator door," the voice says this time.

"Creepy," from girl in green.

"Definitely go tell Lady N, Syd," red says.

Little Syd still looks mighty suspicious, but she nods. "Okay. I will." And she heads down the hallway to the left. The other girls don't move, but it doesn't matter. They're far enough away for Shuri and K'Marah to slip by (hopefully undetected).

"Please step out of the elevator."

And this time, Shuri follows the direction. With a firm pull on K'Marah's arm, they walk out of the elevator and bank left, and Shuri exhales in relief: There's Syd, some twenty meters ahead, bouncing on her toes as she walks with purpose.

Shuri has no idea where they are or how they're going to get out of here, but one thing is for sure: They have to get inside that office.

12

BRIGHT FUTURES

It's a miracle they're able to keep sight of the small, pink-clad girl: There are so many other things vying for their attention, Shuri consistently finds her eyes pulled in various directions. In addition to the delightfully upbeat music wafting through the air—which smells the way it did in the entry hall, but stronger—there are young girls everywhere.

And they all look . . . happy.

As the Wakandan girls walk, careful to avoid bumping into anyone, Shuri wonders if there's any rhyme or reason to the jumpsuit colors. They've come to a bend in the hallway that spits them around a corner to the right. Opposite the corner is a cross hallway that leads down to the left and dead-ends at a wall that looks like the fake-wood ones in the anteroom, and it seems like they're headed for a second corner with an adjacent hallway just ahead.

The wide hallway they're traversing is lined with big windows that give view into a variety of rooms, all with brightly colored walls that appear to match the various jumpsuits. There are classrooms, traditional laboratories, and spaces where large-scale tests and experiments are in progress. In one such space, Shuri can see a group of girls using jetpacks, and in another, there's a domed structure that looks like an anti-gravity pod (based on the person floating inside it). There's also a virtual reality lab.

Shuri and K'Marah continue forward behind Syd, and as they bank around the next corner, they can see inside a space Shuri would've never expected in a facility like this one: It's . . . a spa. There are separate hair and nail salons, and set in the back wall is the entrance to a "Fitness Center," according to the words that arch over the double doorway. "Whoa," Shuri whispers beneath her breath, unable to help herself.

As she stares at the girls moving about inside and breathes in the sweet fragrance of the air, the princess can't deny that she'd really like to shed her invisibility suit and go in. To maybe . . . stay here. And though the thoughts feel only half-formed, Shuri can't ignore the *certainty* of them. None of the girls they've seen so far are in any rush to leave . . .

So why should the princess be?

While on a fundamental level, this bizarre invisible hideaway is exceedingly creepy, the princess can't deny understanding why a person—especially one like her—would want to stick around. A fully supplied research and experimentation facility, full of young people who have no problem whiling the days away in pursuit of knowledge and scientific advancement? Where can she sign up—

A tug on her hand snatches Shuri back from "la-la land," as the queen mother calls it, and her vision clears.

Right on time, too: A pair of young ladies exit into the main hallway—a tall one in a red jumpsuit with brown skin and shoulder-length locs, and a short, curvy one in pink, also brown-skinned, but redheaded and freckled. The taller girl looks more familiar than Shuri is expressly comfortable with, and the princess's pulse picks up pace. When the pair passes the two invisible Wakandans, Shuri catches sight of the tall one's nails as she shows them to her friend. They're painted with images of little gears.

The word *robotics* pops to the top of Shuri's mind, and recognition hits her like a M'Shindi blow to the sternum: Cici. Riri's missing friend from Chicago.

If *she's* here, then . . .

They have to get into that office.

Shuri quickens her pace, pulling K'Marah along with her. But K'Marah trips. And while their basic movements and even her crash to the floor might be silent (at least Shuri thinks they are . . . she only knows K'Marah has gone down because she almost pulls the princess with her), the Dora-in-training's yelp certainly is not.

Syd whips around, and Shuri feels K'Marah scramble back to her feet.

"Who's there?" Syd says, face red. "I know you were in the elevator! You . . . you better show yourself!"

The princess doesn't even breathe.

Syd shuts her eyes and takes a deep breath. (*Oh boy . . . What is she doing?* Shuri thinks.) Then she shoves her hands out in front of her and begins moving in their direction.

The princess is tempted to pull K'Marah to the side so they can flatten themselves against the window to the spa, but with the amount she's perspiring right now, there's a very good chance her body, though invisible, would fog the glass. Maybe she and K'Marah can separate for a second until Syd passes them by—

"Uhhh, Syd?" comes a voice from behind them. Shuri risks a peek over her shoulder. It's the girl in yellow from the entry hall. She's just rounded the corner, and is frozen in place. *Concern* evident in her single raised eyebrow. "You . . . okay?"

"There's somebody there, Britt. I *know* there is."

"I . . . don't see anybody?"

"That's because they're invisible!"

At this, Britt—who looks older than Shuri and K'Marah—sighs. "Come on," she says, striding forward. Shuri spins to face K'Marah, moving out of Britt's path just in time: If not for the mask, she'd be able to feel the air on her cheek as the girl in yellow breezes past. "I'll walk the rest of the way to the office with you," Britt says. "I know the whole elevator thing was disconcerting, but Lady N will get it fixed, okay?" She drapes an arm over the smaller girl's shoulders, spinning her away from Shuri and K'Marah. They continue up the hall toward the next bend.

"We have to catch up to them," Shuri whispers to K'Marah before rotating away and pulling the shorter girl into stride.

When Shuri and K'Marah *do* catch up—they had a couple of dodge-necessary near encounters on the way—Britt and Syd are standing outside a closed door. "Hmm," Britt says with her hands on her hips. "Looks like no one's home, Syd. We'll have to come back."

Syd's shoulders droop before she looks in the direction of the hidden Wakandan girls. They've stopped about four meters away, across from the window to an astronomy lab, if the three massive telescopes along the back wall are any indication. It's Shuri's first time seeing a window in this place . . . which makes her wonder what floor they're on. (How many floors even are there?)

"Come on," Britt goes on, snatching Shuri back. "I'll walk you to your wing. You can show me your latest prototype for your hover train." She extends an elbow, and after a beat of hesitation, Syd grabs on and allows herself to be pulled away from the door.

Once they turn the next corner—and Shuri takes a peek to make sure the hallway is empty—she makes a move toward the door.

And gets tugged back. "What are you doing?" K'Marah hisses. "We can't just keep following—"

"We need to get into the office," Shuri whispers back.

"They just said no one's there."

"Which means it's the perfect time to go in." The princess tries to pull them forward again.

K'Marah doesn't budge. "What if there's an alarm on the door?"

"We're invisible. They already think there's a glitch because of the elevator. If there's an alarm and they find no one, it'll be lumped in with that."

"But what if there are, like . . . heat-sensitive cameras or something? They'll notice us then!"

At this, Shuri huffs. She leans her shoulder into K'Marah's so she can get as close to her friend as possible. "Look: Last I checked, we're only in this place because *you* insisted that we infiltrate. I saw Riri's friend coming out of that spa area earlier, and while I have no idea if the others are here somewhere, we're *in* now and might as well be thorough. You can either come with me, or you can stay here in the hall. Either way, I'm getting into that office. There's no turning back now."

Shuri moves to release K'Marah's hand, but K'Marah doesn't let go. "Fine," she hisses. "But if we get caught and used as test subjects for electricity experiments or something, I'm blaming you."

To Shuri's shock, the door is unlocked and the light is on inside the room. Which, like the entryway and elevator, is shaped like a hexagon. There's an array of six rectangular tables, each one parallel to the wall it's in front of, and a hexagonal desk at the center of the space. (What is it with this place and hexagons?)

Once both girls are inside with the door shut, Shuri stops whispering. "Okay, we're going to split," she says. "Gotta make this fast. You take that half, and I'll take this one." She points.

"Uhhh . . . I take which half? I . . . can't see you."

Oh. Right, Shuri thinks. "If you're facing the wall opposite the door, you take the right side of the room."

"Got it."

Shuri starts at a table with a set of tablets docked on it, but of course she doesn't know the passcodes and can't get any of them to unlock. Even trying to hack them is futile: They're locked down tighter than T'Challa's Kimoyo journal entries. A move to a different table proves beneficial: She finds a schematic diagram of the structure they're in. *The Garden*, it says across the top.

And Shuri can't help but be awed. The place is a science lover's paradise.

The entire edifice is two floors: the one they're on, and a living space with dorm-style rooms one level belowground. And all made up of multiple identical-size hexagons. The floor they're on contains the entryway and elevator, and then beyond it, something called "Hydrogen Hall" that appears to be a theater-style meeting space. Then there are five hexagonal "wings"—biology, chemistry, astronomy, physics, and earth sciences. And all are color-coded. Colors that, if she had to guess, likely correlate with the girls' different jumpsuit hues.

These wings, with the theater as the sixth block, connect and surround a central seventh hexagon that contains mathematics and technology sections as well as something smack in the middle of the facility simply labeled *The Hive*.

And yes: There is a whole spa.

Shuri quickly slips out her Kimoyo card to take a photo.

And then her eyes are drawn to the center of the room, where light is suddenly emanating from the surface of the desk.

The only word Shuri can manage when she reaches the (hexagonal) thing is "Whoa." There's a large screen embedded in the wood, and on said screen—apart from the incoming message notification that caused the screen to illuminate in the first place—is a digitized schematic.

One with labeled dots moving all around it.

The labels include a single letter—an initial, Shuri quickly figures out—followed by a period and three other letters.

Which, knowing what she knows, makes it difficult

to shake the feeling that the *C.Jen* in the engineering and robotics section is *Cici Jenkins*, Riri's friend Shuri thinks she spotted in the hall. The *S.Reh* currently bouncing about in optical astronomy is probably for *Sharleen Rehmann*, the planetary-system-discovering girl missing from Pakistan.

Shuri's eyes drift to the zoology department in the bio wing . . . and there it is: *P.Bau.*

Pilar Bautista.

"Hey, K'Marah? What is your French friend's surna—"

"We have to leave," K'Marah says. There's a sheet of paper seemingly floating in midair. "Like right, right now. Where are you?"

"Huh?"

The sheet slams down on the table. "I can't *see* you. Where are you? We need to *leave*."

Shuri rolls her eyes. "Look, I know you're scared, but—"

"Please just tell me where you are!"

"Fine! Jeez!" Shuri removes her Kimoyo card from the pocket of her suit and holds it in the air.

"Okay, great," K'Marah says, grabbing the paper, rushing over, and reaching for Shuri's hand. "Let's go."

"K'Marah, *wait*." Shuri snatches away. "I need you

to look at this map and tell me if you see your French friends—"

"We need to *go*, Shuri!" K'Marah says. And something about the way she says it this time makes Shuri snap to attention. "Look!" K'Marah shoves the sheet of paper in Shuri's direction, and the princess takes it.

Then she drops it on the floor.

It's a list.

Bright Futures is printed big and bold at the top.

And three spaces down?

Princess Shuri of Wakanda.

13

UNDER ATTACK

With the map of the hexagon-centric facility in hand, locating the emergency exit that will place the Wakandan girls nearest to the *Predator* is easy. The door is at the back end of the purple-coded biology wing, and Shuri knows an alarm is likely to blare once they open it, but by the time anyone responds to the disturbance, she and K'Marah will have slipped out.

But as the girls round the final corner and spot the hallway that will lead them to freedom, one of the girls they saw leaving the spa earlier steps into their path.

Riri's friend Cici.

Shuri doesn't realize she's following the tall girl until she feels a pull on her arm so intense, it makes her suck in a breath. "What are you *doing*?" K'Marah hisses from behind her. "The exit is this way!"

Shuri watches as Cici pauses to hug a friend in passing, and then walks through an automatic door on the right. Shuri peeks at the layout image on her phone. Cici has entered a washroom. "I have to talk to her," she says.

"Talk to *whom*?"

"The girl in red."

"Shuri, I don't think this is a good ide—"

"Come on." And Shuri pulls K'Marah forward.

Once inside the space, Shuri slips into a stall and decloaks herself. When the princess hears the flush of the toilet next door and the *zip* of Cici's jumpsuit, she takes a deep breath. The taller girl's stall creaks open, and there's a sound of footsteps before water is turned on.

Shuri pulls her own stall door wide and steps out. She and Cici lock eyes in the mirror, and Cici's go wide before they narrow. With suspicion.

The princess has to talk fast.

"Umm . . . hi," Shuri says, launching herself forward. She sticks her hand out, and Cici looks down at it. Clearly grossed out.

Shuri bets K'Marah is rolling her eyes right now.

"Sorry, should probably wash that, eh?" Shuri steps up to the sink. "So I know you don't know me, but I know who *you* are because I know a friend of yours? Riri Williams is her name—"

"Wait, you know Riri?" Now the girl just looks confused.

"Yes!" Shuri says, thinking she's found an *in*. "I do! She's . . . been looking for you."

Wrong thing to say. Cici's face shutters instantly and suspicion crawls back into her eyebrows. "Who are you?" she says. "I don't think I've seen you before. Which sci-dis do you belong to?"

"Which . . ." Shuri's vision has begun to go fuzzy at the edges. Is she *that* nervous? "Come again?"

"Sci. Dis. As in scientific discipline?" Cici gives Shuri a once-over. "Why are you out of uniform?"

The longer Shuri stands without her suit's mask on, the harder it becomes to hold her thoughts together. It's as if they all tumble apart into individual letters and leak out her ears.

She actually smiles at the thought.

What is going on?

She shakes her head. The fog clears just enough for Shuri to remember what she's doing here.

"Okay," she says. "I know this is likely very strange,

being accosted in the washroom by a complete stranger within a maximum security facility in the middle of a salt desert, but you have to listen to me, Cici: You are in danger. Everyone here is. Lady N . . . she's not a good person."

To Shuri's utter shock, Cici looks genuinely concerned. And maybe a bit betrayed. "She's not?"

"Nope. Not at all. We have to get you and the others out of here. Before it's too late." (For *what*, exactly, Shuri isn't sure, but she doesn't say that.)

"Wow!" Cici says. "That's . . . wow! Have you told anyone else this? Some authorities have to know, right? Has Riri alerted anyone back home?"

Shuri exhales. This is going better than she expected.

"Ummm . . . Well, I wasn't *completely* sure about things until we arrived."

Cici nods. "Good call," she says.

Shuri feels a tug on the back of her suit, but she ignores it. Gotta seal the deal. "So you'll come?"

"Oh, I definitely want to leave with you, but I need to let a friend know so she can cover for me until we get back with help. Can you wait here?"

Another tug. Shuri ignores.

"Of course, of course." Shuri nods so fervently, it's a wonder her head doesn't detach from her neck and roll across the floor.

The moment Cici exits, Shuri rounds on K'Marah. "Why were you pulling on my suit? Are you trying to get us caught?"

"I don't have a good feeling about this, Shuri," comes a disembodied voice from farther to the right than Shuri expects.

"What has gotten into you? Aren't *I* usually the overly cautious one?"

"I'm wondering the same thing about you."

"What do you mean?"

In truth, Shuri has a vague idea of precisely what K'Marah means, but she can't seem to hold it in her head. All she can currently think about is how pretty the music is and how good the air smells.

The princess would love to tour the engineering and tech sections of this place, and is sad that she won't be able to. In fact, Shuri finds that she is mildly envious of anyone who gets to stay here.

"I'll admit that, yes, I *have* been feeling off, but you . . . you've been a bit *rash* since we entered this place," K'Marah continues. "Frankly, I'm surprised that you trust that girl. She agreed a bit too *swiftly*, in my opinion . . . In fact, we should probably leave before she comes back. *If* she comes back."

"You are being such a . . . a *Deckie Downer*."

"It's *Debbie* Downer. And I'm not trying to be,

Shuri. I just . . . something isn't right. At least go back invisible in case someone else comes in—"

A siren sound begins to blare.

"*Warning: intruder alert. Building lockdown commencing.*"

K'Marah doesn't say anything else, but she doesn't have to. Shuri feel the waves of *I told you so* flowing off her invisible best friend in time with the alarm. The princess returns to invisibility . . .

And just in time: The door to the bathroom swings open, and an older girl—maybe college-age?—sticks her head in. Her jumpsuit is black. "Don't bother," comes a voice from behind her. "I'm sure she fled the moment the alarm went off."

The older girl's eyes sweep the room before she disappears back into the hallway. And then Shuri is yanked forward with so much force, she lets out a small yelp. (The alarm is still blaring, praise Bast.)

"Sorry," K'Marah says, not bothering to whisper *or* ease up on her pulling. "We have to catch that door while it's still open to slip out unnoticed."

And they do . . . but the hallway is utter mayhem.

"*Warning: intruder alert. Lockdown in progress.*"

Shuri and K'Marah are positioned directly across from the hallway that leads to the emergency exit, but there are too many girls zipping left and right in front of them. Like a bunch of human gumballs in a high entropy state.

They toss inquiries back and forth through the air.

"She's not in the theater?"

"What did Jenkins say she looked like, again?"

"Where the heck could someone even *hide* in this place?"

"A hazmat suit? She was wearing a purple hazmat suit?"

And then there's a break in the traffic.

Thankfully K'Marah notices, too. They take off across the wide gap and bolt down the narrower hallway up the center of the bio wing.

(And despite the danger—and the glaring red lights flashing overhead—it's impossible for the princess not to peek into the subsections: botany and zoology on the left, human and microbiology on the right.)

It seems as though they're headed toward a dead end. A wall. Like the one in the entry area—painted to look like wood, with a panel across the center containing a double-helix carving. But then that wretched voice rings out again: *"Warning: intruder alert. Lockdown complete."* And the outline of a hidden door flashes before the girls.

They race to it, feeling around for some sort of handle or hidden lever. "Come onnnnnn," K'Marah says, hitting the wall (door?) with her fist. Nothing.

"We're doomed," Shuri says, leaning her forehead against it.

"Uh-oh . . ." K'Marah's voice says beside the princess.

Shuri turns, fully prepared to shout *"I KNOW IT'S ALL OVER!"* in her best friend's invisible face (and she calls K'Marah dramatic). But K'Marah hisses again: "Someone's looking this way."

Shuri slowly peeks over her shoulder (then remembers no one can see her and feels exceedingly silly). "Oh my gods," she says. There, with her head sticking out of the zoology and botany room and looking *right* at the spot where Shuri and K'Marah are standing, is a girl Shuri instantly recognizes:

Pilar Bautista.

Her jumpsuit is purple.

After a glance in the opposite direction, Pilar steps out of the room and begins to creep in the direction of the Wakandan girls. On tiptoe.

Which is . . . odd.

Shuri lets go of K'Marah's hand and flattens herself against the glass wall to her right, hoping K'Marah is doing the same. Once Pilar reaches the wall/door, she takes one final gander behind her before heaving a sigh, and running a hand across the double-helix carving.

"The facility is in an active lockdown. Please return to your dormitory," comes that Bast-awful voice. (Shuri hates it, hates it, hates it.)

"Oh no, oh no—"

"Pilar?" comes a voice from the far end of the hall (though it seems to have shortened). There's another, older girl in a black jumpsuit, this one potentially of Latin descent. "*¿Qué pasa?* You don't hear the alarm?"

"Oh, uhhh . . . I thought I heard something else," Pilar replies. "Thought I would check the door to see if the intruder went out this way."

From the way the older girl's eyes narrow, it would be evident to anyone watching that she doesn't believe Pilar for a single second. But she just nods. "Did you find anything?"

"No." Pilar's chin drops. Shuri has no idea what comes over her, but she wants to reach out and lift the younger girl's head back up. She's *almost* close enough to do so. "The door had locked."

The older girl nods. "All right. Come on, then."

Despite Shuri's level of perturbation—Pilar was *clearly* trying to escape—watching her go to the girl in black as summoned gives the princess an idea.

"Shuri?" K'Marah's voice sounds more panicked than the princess has ever heard it.

"I'm here, I'm here," Shuri replies. "Keep a lookout, will you?"

"Uhhh . . ."

At this, Shuri pulls her Kimoyo card from her pocket—praying to the Orisha that she can get a signal inside the Garden—and she summons the *Predator*. Takes a few tries, but eventually, the princess's beloved craft is hovering invisibly just beyond the locked door.

"Cover your ears," Shuri whispers to K'Marah.

And then she fires the *Predator*'s sound cannon. A weapon that's really no weapon at all. More a scare tactic. The noise sounds like something much more terrifying than what amounts to little more than a forced—and non-damaging—miniature sonic boom.

"*Warning: The facility is under attack. Please evacuate.*"

And the emergency exit unlocks with a faint *click*. K'Marah removes her hand from her suit's glove (Shuri hopes she'll be able to erase the image of her friend's disembodied, floating appendage from memory) and runs her glitter-polished fingertips over the double-helix carving like Pilar had done.

The door slides open with a hiss. "Yes!" Shuri shouts. "Freedom!"

She and K'Marah rush out . . . and discover a new

problem: The Garden girls truly *are* evacuating. Which means the Wakandan royal and her guard-in-training can't reveal themselves so they can see each other.

Nor can Shuri reveal the *Predator* so the pair can get inside it.

MISSION LOG

WELL, THAT WAS ALMOST A DISASTER.

I wound up having to use the Kimoyo capture mechanism to fly us far enough away—dangling beneath the *Predator* in terrifying (and nauseating) electro-magnetic spheres—to avoid being seen.

On a positive note: I do believe the gods decided we'd had enough trouble for one day, because when we got back to Clothier Lwazi, he seemed more frazzled than when we left, but he wasn't angry, and he promised not to rat us out. "I wasn't born yesterday, darlings," he said. "While my dear niece does have a bit of style sense, the fact that *you*, Princess, requested an international fabric-shopping trip was quite suspect. I figured you'd scurry off at some point. Though I would be a liar if I said I wasn't worried you wouldn't come back."

He lay down for the duration of the flight.

All in all, despite what we discovered, I need some time to process and refocus. Come up with a plan. Because one thing is abundantly clear: None of those girls appeared to be occupants of the Garden against their wills. Pilar's anomaly of a seeming escape attempt aside, they all seemed to be . . . enjoying themselves.

I can't say I am entirely sure what to make of that.

Or of the sight of my name on that list.

14

DOUBT

Returning to business-as-usual is impossible.

Internally, at least.

Externally, Shuri gets back to work: training harder than ever, studying, being precisely where she's supposed to be, precisely when she's supposed to be there.

She tries to keep herself convinced that her sole priority is still earning her way to that conclave with T'Challa, and anyone watching her would believe that to be the case.

But in truth, where the whole missing-girls mystery

previously distracted her from Panther training, now the two have flipped: Training is keeping her distracted from thinking about the girls. Which is why she does so much of it her first few days back from her and K'Marah's Ethiopian desert jaunt.

In fact, on day three, M'Shindi permits Shuri to make up her missed assessment. And the princess nails it. She even manages to completely disarm the older woman, a feat not even her darling brother ever accomplished.

Her mother looks none too pleased when she hears.

Try though she might, however, Shuri can't seem to get excited about her triumphs. The conclave is one week hence, and if her mother booking Shuri an appointment with the clothier is any indication—*"So you'll have something proper to wear if you wind up going to this* thing *your brother intends to drag you to"*—Shuri has almost succeeded in her mission.

So why isn't she . . . if not *exuberant*, at least moderately happy?

It's not as though thinking about the other thing is bringing the princess any sense of joy or purpose, either. In fact, part of her motivation behind *avoiding* thoughts of what she and K'Marah discovered is that when Shuri *tries* to think of the Garden, her memories of the place blur at the edges.

It is the most bizarre thing. More than a couple of times, Shuri has attempted to record her memories, thoughts, and feelings, but when she tries to write, she comes up empty. She remembers lots of glass, but not what she saw beyond it. A wide hallway that bent at strange angles, but not what it led to. A carving of a double helix, but not what surrounded it. Girls in multi-hued jumpsuits, but not which colors.

She even printed the photo she snapped of the Garden's layout and has, on three occasions, made an effort to jot down whatever comes to mind when she looks at it. And though her memories are vivid when her eyes are on the image, the second her fingers touch down on a keyboard, everything goes blurry. Same with a pen. There was even an attempt to stare at the picture and do an audio recording. Also a no-go: She's not sure how long she tried to speak, but all that could be heard on playback was "Uhhh . . ."

The few times Shuri has seen K'Marah—in Upanga during training—the girls have barely made eye contact. And they certainly haven't spoken. Shuri's not entirely sure why, but the thought of trying to have a conversation with her best friend about *anything* right now is . . . she just can't do it. No matter what they would discuss—some new roundhouse kick technique, what they had for breakfast, the latest fashion

Shuri has no clue about—the princess knows the discourse would be weighed down by what they *aren't* discussing. And she can't bring herself to talk about the thing she really wants to because . . . well, when Shuri tries to think of what she would say, she can't get any words to form.

It's confusing. And frustrating.

And the worst part: When Shuri *is* able to see the place clearly—typically at night, right as she hits that strange liminal space between fully awake and sound asleep—the thing she remembers most? How *fun* the Garden seemed. How inviting. How nice the scent in the air and how perfect the music (which consistently gets stuck inside her head on a loop). How welcoming it would be for a girl like her. Would her mother allow her to go to a place like that? Even for a brief time? Her name *was* on that list . . . Does *Bright Futures* mean "next in line to receive an invitation"?

In these times, she can't help but wonder if none of the girls have been reported missing because their loved ones know exactly where they are. And that they are thriving there.

It's the reason she's been dodging Riri's calls and hasn't told the other girl that she not only knows where Cici is, but also spoke with her. Cici clearly had zero interest in leaving the Garden: She's the one who sounded the intruder alarm.

Yes: Something doesn't feel *quite* right about the place—seems strange to hide what is essentially a girl-centric innovation lab and not to allow the girls invited there to tell their friends where they are. And Shuri definitely can't shake the feeling that Pilar Bautista was trying to get out (which is a red flag if there ever was one) . . .

But as much as something inside Shuri *wants* to lean into the sense of wrongness, she can't. In fact, though she tries to resist the sentiment, there's a small voice in her head, sound tracked by that amazing music, suggesting *Pilar* is the problem.

In fact, the only time Shuri *really* feels like there's something sinister about the place is when her favorite song—an upbeat, percussion-heavy tune about girls running the world—filters into her still-sleeping mind in the form of an alarm each morning. It's then that she's overcome with a sense of urgency to *do* something. But when she wakes fully, that urgency gets stifled by . . . well, she's not entirely sure what.

This morning is no different.

As the words *Who run the world?* drift into Shuri's ears, something inside her seizes up, and her mind whirs into action trying to figure out how she can set all those girls free. Because they are clearly trapped there, and whoever this Lady N is, she definitely has sinister plans that do *not* take the girls' well-being into consideration. (The princess doesn't know *how* she knows this, but she's *certain* it's the truth.) She *must* act—

"Shuri!" comes a voice that makes the princess's arm hairs stand up straighter than the Dora Milaje in flank formation. "Oh, gods help me," the voice continues, exasperated now. "Shuri!" There's a shake of Shuri's shoulder. "Why are you not out of bed, child?"

The song continues to play.

"Shuri!" Then: "What is this American nonsense . . . ?"

The song cuts off.

"Wake. UP, child!"

Shuri cracks one eye. Her mother is standing over her bed, arms crossed. The absurdly long and ornate lace sleeves of her royal-blue gown hang down her front like fabric waterfalls. And *she* looks ready to explode. Like a geyser. The thought of her tall blue hat shooting off her head with water beneath it makes Shuri grin.

"You think this amusing, do you?" Her mother swats at Shuri's hip. "You feel that our beloved cloth-ier has little else to do than wait for you to decide you are ready to grace him with your presence? Is that how you feel?"

Right. The fitting her mother scheduled.

Her mother swats again.

"Ow!" Shuri says, shifting away. "I'm up, I'm up." She rubs her eyes with the heels of her hands.

Which just sets her mother off even more. "Stop that at once or you will damage your optic nerve, child! Tuh! I wonder what your dear brother would say if he knew his 'escort' to this *conclave* lacks the decency to arrive on time to a fitting for the clothes she needs to go!"

"*Okay*, Mother. I'm sorry!" Shuri sits up and perches at the edge of the bed.

"The clothier is the person you owe an apology!"

"And I will give him one five minutes from now"— she yawns—"when I reach his quarters."

"The nerve of you young people," the queen says, spinning on the pointy toe of a jewel-encrusted slipper and making her way to the door. "Five minutes. Or you will be barred from visiting that laboratory of yours for the remainder of the month."

"Mother!"

"Five minutes, Shuri."

Just like that, the Garden returns to Shuri's consciousness as a place that doesn't seem all that bad.

Especially in comparison with *this* one.

At the four minutes and fifty-two seconds mark, Shuri stumbles into Clothier Lwazi's workshop, completely out of breath.

Of course her mother isn't even there. (Must parents be so endlessly annoying?)

"She lives!" Lwazi says from the opposite end of the room where he is pinning cloth into a headless mannequin.

"Apologies for my tardiness, sir."

"Mm-hmm," he replies without turning around. "That is what they all say. Go ahead and step up onto the dais."

Shuri walks to the center of the room and climbs the two steps to the brightly lit platform. There are mirrored alcoves all along the front and back walls for trying things on and examining them from multiple angles. So unless Shuri wants to stand facing the door—which the clothier would certainly balk at—she's forced to see herself reflected many times over and from myriad directions. It's disorienting and deeply uncomfortable. Especially considering that as of right now, the princess is not entirely sure who she even is.

Or what she wants.

"You've not been sleeping well, either, I see," Lwazi

says as he approaches with a stretch of shimmering indigo fabric draped over his arm. "You girls and these *adventures* of yours. Feet apart, please."

At the sound of the words *either* and *girls*, a knot forms in Shuri's chest. She's been doing her best not to think about the crime she and her dearly beloved partner-in-trespassing committed (among other things).

"Now, I know you despise dresses, but the queen would have my head *and* hands if we didn't at least *mimic* a look of traditional feminine elegance. So we're going to do a nice utility cocoon pant with an elasticized hem and lots of hidden pockets," he continues, placing a stretch of measuring tape from Shuri's waist to her left ankle. "My, how you girls have grown."

He steps around to Shuri's front. "For the top, we'll do a fitted bodice with a sheer turtle-style neckline and long sleeves."

"Okay" is all Shuri says.

"Arms out."

Shuri complies, and the measuring tape is first stretched from wrist to wrist, then dropped and wrapped around her waist.

"All right," Clothier Lwazi says, stepping down to the floor. "Away with you."

Shuri opens her mouth to speak, but thinks better of it. Lamenting what a waste of time this was isn't likely to land her anywhere good, especially considering that the clothier didn't tattle on them. "Thank you, sir" is all she says. She descends as well and heads for the door.

"Mm-hmm. I will send for you in a few days' time."

"Okay."

Shuri has almost reached the door when Lwazi calls out to her again.

"Princess?"

Her heart clenches, and she freezes on the spot. "Yes, sir?"

"A favor?"

She shuts her eyes. "Yes, sir?"

"Check in with your dear friend, will you? You both look downright dreadful, and your shared well-being is of concern to me. Especially considering the hours I spent navigating *crowds* in Ethiopia."

Shuri doesn't respond.

"Alone," he continues.

"Yes, Clothier."

"I am placing the responsibility with you because between the two of us, your inner strength surpasses that of my niece. I have no interest in what the pair of you got up to when you left me behind, but if there is something *wrong* with either of you, I will have no choice but to intervene."

Shuri takes a deep breath. "Understood, sir."

"Excellent. I'm sure you loves will work things out. Enjoy the rest of your day!"

"Yes, sir."

And Shuri exits the room before the lump in her chest moves up into her throat and spills out her eyes.

15

FAILURE

But the princess doesn't keep her word.

In fact, she doubles down on her avoidance of K'Marah. For the next couple of days, Shuri spends just about every waking hour—and even a handful of sleeping ones—holed up in her laboratory, studying like her very life depends on it. The song from the Garden thankfully begins to fade, so she's able to focus without fuzzy recollections of the place invading her thoughts, and with three exams to ace within three days, no one questions Shuri's semi-reclusive behavior.

Well . . . almost no one.

"Shuri, have you spoken with K'Marah as of late?" Nakia asks the moment Shuri breaks for a mid-afternoon snack on day two of hide-and-cram. The Dora is sitting on one of the leather couches Shuri had added to what has essentially become a sitting area in the lab space. There's even a coffee table made from the salvaged wood of a formerly poisoned border forest tree (shout-out to K'Marah's ex-flame, Henbane) covered in American fashion magazines pilfered from Clothier Lwazi.

"Hmm?" Shuri says, freezing on the spot almost directly behind the Dora.

"K'Marah," Nakia replies, turning a page in a periodical called *Elle*. "You two *are* still good friends, yes? Or did I miss something?"

For reasons beyond Shuri's comprehension, her heart begins to race. "Umm . . . yes. We are." She unsticks her feet and walks as quickly as she can to the kitchen without seeming like she's attempting to flee the conversation (which . . . she is).

"Ah. Good," Nakia goes on. "So you can tell me what's *really* going on with her, then? I don't want to pry, but I'm beginning to worry."

The princess is very happy there is a wall between them now: It prevents Nakia from being able to see

Shuri's face. "What . . ." Shuri gulps, ". . . are you worried about, exactly?"

"We haven't seen her since your shared trip to Ethiopia. Word on the Upanga mats is that she's ill. Picked up some sort of norovirus during your trip to Ethiopia. Is that true?"

Oh Bast. Is Shuri really about to lie outright *again*? She takes a deep breath. "Yes. It, umm . . . took a while to air out my travel vessel, in fact. The stench was horrific."

"Ah," Nakia says. "So . . . how do you think you managed to avoid it?"

Uh-oh. "Hmm?"

"You are clearly familiar with norovirus, so my assumption is that you know how contagious it is, Princess," Nakia says. "I can understand your not contracting it from the same source as K'Marah, but you two surely had enough contact for her to pass it on to you. The clothier also seems to have escaped unscathed. Which is . . . unusual."

"Oh. Umm . . ." But Shuri can't come up with a single thing to say.

"The next time you speak with her, please let her know we send our well wishes and are concerned. No one has been able to get in contact with her since—"

But an alert chime rings through the air.

And as thankful as Shuri is that it cuts her conversation with Nakia short, she's none too thrilled with what it means: There's a new hit on the P.R.O.W.L. network.

Convincing Nakia to "take a fiver" so Shuri can listen to the transcript in private might be the most difficult thing the princess has done in the past week. She had to stoop to issuing a royal command, which obligated the Dora to comply without question. Her face was steel on the way out into the cave corridor. (If the warrior wasn't suspicious enough about what might *really* be going on with the princess and her Dora-in-training friend, she certainly is now.)

After cursing herself for forgetting to turn the network off the minute she entered the lab, Shuri sits down in front of her computer screen. The transcript is short, but she can't bring herself to read it. She presses the button to play the recording and braces herself for the worst.

ALERT: KEYWORD *JOSEPHINE DUBOIS*
LOCATION: KAMPALA, UGANDA
TIME: 15:22
TRANSCRIPTION:
 "...*JOSEPHINE DUBOIS* RECOMMENDED THIS RECRUIT YOU SAY?"

"CORRECT. SHE CLAIMS TO HAVE [UNABLE TO TRANSCRIBE] HERE SOME TIME AGO [UNABLE TO TRANSCRIBE] TECH SUMMIT."

"AHA. AND [UNABLE TO TRANSCRIBE] THE YOUNG LADY'S SPECIALTY?"

"ADVANCED COMBAT AND [UNABLE TO TRANSCRIBE]."

"HMM...I GUESS THAT COULD COME IN HANDY. AND SHE IS LOCATED [UNABLE TO TRANSCRIBE] KAMPALA?"

"NO, MADAM. WE ARE HERE BECAUSE [UNABLE TO TRANSCRIBE] LAST POINT OF CONTACT. THIS RECRUIT IS...DIFFERENT. IT IS IMPERATIVE THAT WE GATHER MORE INTEL BEFORE [UNABLE TO TRANSCRIBE]."

"I SEE. BUT YOU *DO* KNOW *WHERE* [UNABLE TO TRANSCRIBE]?"

"WE DO. SHE IS IN [UNABLE TO TRANSCRIBE]...APPROXIMATELY 900 KILOMETERS NORTHEAST."

"REALLY? DOES THIS MEAN [UNABLE TO TRANSCRIBE] TWO RECRUITS FROM [UNABLE TO TRANSCRIBE]?"

"MY THINKING IS THAT WE RECRUIT HER INSTEAD [UNABLE TO TRANSCRIBE] MUCH TOO HIGH-PROFILE."

Shuri puts her forehead on the desk. Not because she's *too* terribly troubled by what she just heard (at least there's not a *new* girl missing ... yet). More because she knows the name *Josephine* all too well.

She has no choice now: She *has* to find and speak to K'Marah.

The door buzzes as Nakia returns from her break, and Shuri lets her in.

"Did you complete whatever NSIFOG scheme you were working on?" she says, clearly still miffed over being bossed around by an early adolescent.

"NSIFOG?"

"Not safe in front of grown-ups."

Shuri clears her throat and stands to gather her things. "I have no idea what you're talking about, Nakia."

"Mm-hmm. It was clearly enough to drag your face out of all those textbooks. Seems it was also enough to persuade your exit from this den of experimental bliss?"

"Shh."

"Is that a *royal command*, Princess?"

Shuri sighs and slings her knapsack over her shoulder. "You're never going to let me live that down, are you?"

"Nope," Nakia says.

They walk in silence up to the cave entrance, and once they're inside Nakia's miniature hovercraft, Shuri opens her mouth to speak—

But apparently doesn't need to. "We are headed to the mines, I suppose?"

"Huh?"

"You intend to visit your dear friend, do you not?"

Shuri is stunned. "But how—"

"I wasn't born yesterday, Princess. Your lack of vomiting and all the *other* unpleasant manifestations of a true norovirus lead me to believe our beloved K'Marah is lacking these symptoms as well. And while I don't appreciate your secrecy—or you bossing me around—I do very much appreciate your checking on her."

They fall silent, and within seven minutes, Shuri is exiting Nakia's craft and headed up the glistening asphalt walkway (she's always wondered how they manage to keep it so shiny) to the long, sleek house where K'Marah lives.

Not only is she permitted entrance without question, K'Marah's mother, whom Shuri is shocked to see at home, is *so* thrilled about the princess's visit, she pulls Shuri into a hug that practically crushes her small bones.

"Ohhhhh!" the woman howls in Shuri's ear. "My, how you have *grown*!" She lets go.

Shuri clears her throat. "It is wonderful to see you, too, Auntie. Things are good in the mines?"

"Why, yes, they *are*, Your Majesty." With a playful bow.

It embarrasses Shuri. (What will she do if she ever *does* have to rule this nation? Deferential elders are almost too much for Shuri's order-bound mind to handle.) "Umm . . . might I pay K'Marah a visit?"

At this, the woman's face—which is a glowing, slightly more mature version of K'Marah's—morphs from delight to deep concern. "She is quite ill, as I'm sure you're aware. We, ahh . . ." She looks over her shoulder at the closed door to K'Marah's bedroom. "Well, she has insisted on that door remaining closed so 'nothing gets out,' as she put it."

Shuri nods. Whatever is going on with her best friend—and she is now 100 percent certain K'Marah is *not* ill because if she were, the girl would insist on being catered to around the clock—Shuri needs to find out. Perhaps hearing about this ping on her French friend's name and trying to decipher what it means will give K'Marah the resolve to come out of her room.

"The incubation period for contagion should be over," Shuri says, talking utter nonsense as she heads to the door. "And I took some Vibranium-enhanced elderberry, so I should be immune."

"Whatever you say, dear!"

Shuri takes a deep inhale before turning the knob, and then she slips in, quickly shutting the door behind her.

"Go away unless you want everything you eat and drink to exit both ends of you simultaneously," comes a voice from the midst of what appears to be a pile of blankets on the bed.

Shuri rolls her eyes before letting them roam the dim room. It's been so long since she's been here—K'Marah typically comes to *her*—she forgot how over-the-top the space is: The ceiling is swathed with gauzy fabric that Shuri knows will illuminate with fairy lights if she flips the correct switch on the wall. There's a small sitting area in the corner complete with tufted ottomans and ultra-plush chairs that practically suck the sitter down into their depths. ("Memory foam!" K'Marah once told her. "It's all the rage in America.") And the bed Shuri's dear friend has exiled herself to? It's canopy-style and even wider than Shuri's, draped with an iridescent green lace that makes one feel lost in an enchanted forest whenever the panels aren't tied to the four posts.

"K'Marah, you have to get up," Shuri says from her post near the door. She'd love to say the possibility of

K'Marah *truly* being ill is what keeps her rooted to the spot . . . but there's something else, too. A trepidation Shuri couldn't name if she tried.

"Shuri?" The lump shifts. "Is that you?"

"Yes. Now come. I know you're not really sick."

"It's too hard," K'Marah says.

Shuri's nervousness kicks up a notch. "What do you mean?"

The lump groans.

"Listen, you have to get up and help me. There was a ping on your friend's name in Uganda. We need to investigate."

"It's like the color has drained out of everything, Shuri. I can't get the music out of my head."

That certainly gets Shuri's attention. "The music?"

"From that place. I've been having these dreams about it. Those girls there . . . we're all doomed. There's no point."

Shuri gulps. "You . . . you just need some fresh air, is all," she says. "Something to shift your focus—"

"You're going to leave," K'Marah says.

"What? No, I'm not—"

"You are." And K'Marah sits up.

Shuri draws back. She's never seen her friend look so . . . not put together. K'Marah's braids have been removed, and her coily hair is dry and sticking straight up on one side. It'd be a funny sight if not for the deep-set bags beneath the young Dora's eyes. Eyes that are quite red.

"Your name was on that list, Shuri. Don't you see? Your invitation will come just like Josephine's did. And then you'll be gone."

Shuri just blinks. It seems intensely foolish, but it hadn't really clicked that her name on that list could *really* mean what K'Marah is suggesting.

What if Shuri *does* receive an invitation to the Garden?

At the lack of response, K'Marah reburies herself in her mound of blankets. "'Investigate' all you want," she says. "Josephine isn't coming back. And when it's your turn, you won't, either."

16

SISINDISIWE

All Shuri can manage when Nakia returns to retrieve her: "K'Marah really is quite sick." And the look on the princess's face must send a message of its own because the senior-level Dora Milaje doesn't ask a single question.

Attempting to return to her studies is an exercise in futility, but Shuri can't figure out what to do instead. Reaching out to Riri seems the most logical thing. Would probably be a good thing to prevent another disappearance while they have the chance . . .

If they still have the chance. Maybe the invitation

has already been extended and accepted. Would that mean Shuri's is coming next?

The princess isn't sure she's ever been so . . . conflicted.

K'Marah was right about one thing: Now that Shuri is paying attention, she must admit that everything around her *does* seem duller. For instance, she can tell that it's a bright, clear day outside. But the usual brilliance of the sky feels muted to the princess. The trees seem duller. The miners they pass, vaguely ashen. Or does Shuri only feel that way now because K'Marah said so?

"Are you quite all right, Princess?" Nakia says as they approach the palace grounds. "Forgive my impropriety, but you look as though you've seen a ghost. Is K'Marah doing *that* poorly?"

"Oh, umm . . . I'm sure she will be back to normal within a few days' time."

Because Shuri can't bring herself to voice what she *really* feels: fear that she'll never see her "normal" best friend again.

After dinner—and under the guise of further study—Shuri convinces T'Challa to grant her permission to return to her laboratory. Once there, the princess immerses herself in the one thing that never fails to keep her focused: experimenting. First she dismantles a pair of VR helmets she created so she can remove the comm systems from within them. Not that she has any intention of *using* the jumpsuits she and K'Marah wore into the Garden anytime soon, but if she *were* going to, the ability to communicate—especially while in Invisi-mode—would certainly come in handy.

Once she has the ear and mouthpieces in place, she also decides to attach the latest CatEyez prototype to the headpiece she adds to the inside of the suits' hoods.

When those upgrades are finished, Shuri decides to try something she's considered, but been afraid to do. Using the network information that saved to her Kimoyo card when she took that picture of the Garden's layout, Shuri logs onto her desktop computer . . . and attempts to hack into the place.

It's locked down tighter than Wakanda's vault of relics. Which contains a golf ball–size chunk of radioactive Vibranium said to be capable of leveling the continents of North *and* South America simultaneously.

Without making a single sound.

("Why do we even have it?" Shuri remembers asking Baba when he told her about it. She was four years old and had just begun her own experiments with the mysterious celestial substance. He'd smiled down at her. "My dear, if you come up with any bright ideas for how to get rid of the thing, I will be all ears.")

When she's unable to make any virtual headway, Shuri pores over the printed image of the layout itself. While the design of the place itself is nothing short of remarkable, examining the different sections does stir a bizarre combination of questions and longing for the princess. Like what exactly is in "the Hive" section at the Garden's core? Could that be the structure's power source? A control center for all the tech? Would there be a way to access all this from the outside?

And speaking of "tech," what must that section be like? She and K'Marah could see into the biology, chemistry, and astronomy wings as they passed them, but "technology" is housed behind the spa. It can be accessed by walking through the engineering wing, but the only other point of access is through the Hive.

Though perhaps she can get there now. Because where one moment, Shuri is sitting in her lab, the next, she's staring at a reflection of nothing.

Another mirrored panel glides open behind her.

"You have arrived. Please step out of the elevator," says a disembodied voice that makes the princess's skin prickle.

She slowly turns around. The hallway in front of her is now empty.

"Please step out of the elevator."

"K'Marah?" Shuri whispers, though she has a hunch she doesn't need to. "Are you here?"

There's no response.

"Please step out—"

"Fine, fine," the princess hisses. "I'm going!"

Once she hears the elevator door slip shut, she turns right, intending to head the way she and K'Marah *didn't* go when they were last here. She can see to where the hallway banks left, but beyond that is hazy. Like the space is filled with fog.

She proceeds forward cautiously. The music floats through the air, but is muffled. Like a pillow is being held over the speaker. As she approaches the bend, the fog thickens. Which, fine, would typically be a bit of a red flag. But right now, it's like she can't help but keep going.

Shuri shuts her eyes just before stepping into it, and when she opens them—

She's back in Lady N's hexagonal office, standing at the table K'Marah visited first. On that table is the list: *Bright Futures*. And on the list, just as before, is Shuri's name.

"Shuri?" a voice says, and her head snaps up, panic locking around her chest and squeeeeeeezing. She's still very much alone in the office, but when she looks down at the list again, her name has begun to blur.

"Shuri . . ." the voice comes again, more insistent. But the princess doesn't look up this time. She's too entranced by the slow disappearance of her name and something taking form in its place. Another name, she assumes. But she can't quite make it out—

"SHURI!"

The princess jerks awake. Ayo is standing above her with a hand on her shoulder. "My dear, I think it's time we get you home."

Except after that dream, *home* doesn't feel . . . right.

Nothing does.

All night, Shuri tosses and turns in the bed she usually cannot wait to dive into. Her quarters feel alternately too hot and too cold, and the palace itself is suddenly too large.

When Shuri *does* manage to drift off into fitful bouts of half sleep, her dreams are dreadful and dis-jointed. Though a couple involve the Garden and images of her name blurring off that list, the majority are more foreboding. There's one where a man with a metal hand infiltrates the vault of relics and steals the world's most dangerous chunk of Vibranium. One where all the girls at the Garden have been turned into mindless, red-eyed shells of themselves and are plan-ning a global takeover.

One where there's an ambush awaiting T'Challa at that conclave, and Shuri doesn't realize it until it's too late. One where a haggard old woman Shuri recognizes as a well-known seer in the marketplace grows and grows in front of Shuri's eyes before shouting, "*Sisindisiwe!*" and disintegrating.

It's this word and its meaning—*Save us!*—clanging around in Shuri's head when she jolts awake (again).

And realizes she's overslept. Which is definitely not good: Her Global Diplomacy examination is set to begin in twelve minutes.

It's all downhill from there: She accidentally puts pimple cream on her toothbrush (blegh). She collides with a guard while attempting to run out of the palace and catches a gnarly elbow to the ribs. She gets caught in the seat belt while trying to exit Nakia's hovercraft and goes sprawling. And when she stumbles into Scholar M'Walimu's classroom, the (prehistoric) man gives her a once-over before the corners of his mouth turn down. "Tardy *and* unpresentable." Which is when Shuri looks and sees that she's still in her pajama trousers, and is wearing two different shoes.

For the first time in her life—though the sickly smug fossil of a professor makes it clear that "*it certainly won't be the last*"—Shuri fails an exam.

Thinking it will help clear her head, the princess

decides to walk back to the palace. Reacquaint herself with the city she calls home in hopes that it will pull her to center. It takes some convincing, but Nakia agrees to fly overhead so the princess can walk alone.

And it does help. As the princess roams the streets of Birnin Zana, taking in the loud noises and bright colors, admiring the lines and curves of what she knows is some of the most amazing architecture in the world, and looking into the beautiful faces of her fellow Wakandans—with her favorite song about girls running the world flowing into her ears—she begins to remember how much her home means to her.

How much she wants her legacy to be tied to protecting it and the people who live here.

But then she turns down an alleyway that will spit her out near the back gate to the palace, and Nakia's voice cuts through her music. "You're being trailed, Your Majesty," she says. "Elderly woman with a walking staff. I'm certain she is harmless, and if not, I've no doubt you can handle yourself. But I thought you should know."

On instinct, Shuri looks over her shoulder.

And finds herself looking into the face of the old seer woman from her dream.

Shuri freezes, and she and the woman lock eyes as the princess's stomach tumbles into her socks. The last time a person she saw in a dream appeared in real life, it was bad news: Princess Zanda of Narobia, who was out to decimate the heart-shaped herb and destroy Wakanda. The dream *this* older woman appeared in wasn't *too* foreboding, but still.

They're far enough apart for the princess to make a run for it, but she can't seem to move.

The woman opens her mouth and barely breathes out a word . . . but the princess hears it as though it was spoken right into her ear at full volume:

Sisindisiwe.

Save us.

Shuri's entire body goes ice-cold.

And then an alarm rings out.

17
GONE

At the sound, Shuri breaks into a sprint in the direction of the palace.

"Shuri—!"

"I know!" the princess shouts in response to Nakia's voice in her ear. Not that the Dora can hear her. Shuri just hopes her escort sees her running and gets the message: *NO TIME TO TALK JUST GET TO THE PALACE.*

Because that alarm? It's a *nation*wide one. *The* nationwide one. The one that denotes an incoming invasion or natural disaster.

Shuri is fully focused now.

She just saw the woman from one of her recent dreams . . . could a different one also be coming true? Has the colonizer-complected man with the metal hand—Baba's killer, Klaw, she now realizes—breeched their borders and somehow made his way underground to the vault? Have all those bright and brilliant minds gone rogue, and now there's an army of girl geniuses on the verge of launching an attack? Whoever's behind the Garden's operation obviously knows of Wakanda's existence if Shuri's name was on that list . . . what if Shuri's dream about her name being blotted off that list was actually a sign that Lady N (or whoever) wants *her*—Princess Shuri of Wakanda—blotted out of existence?

Shuri flies down the rear driveway to the palace and up the marble steps to the back doors that will deposit her in the kitchens.

It's mayhem inside the large space. Aproned—and some vibrantly chef-hatted—staff members pushing, shoving, and shouting as they flow into the hallway and head toward the nearest stairwell that will lead down to the palace's bunker. Shuri weaves her way through the bodies and runs in the opposite direction of the foot traffic.

She zips past the main ballroom and hangs left at

the back of the grand foyer, then jets straight up a long marble hallway and across the formal dining hall lined with portraits of Wakanda's kings. If Shuri didn't know better, she'd swear the one of Baba is watching her.

She shoulders through the secret panel beneath her great-great-grandfather's beaming face, and stumbles into the low-lit concrete passageway that leads to the palace's security center. As Shuri approaches the small room, she sees a cadre of guards clumped around the open entrance. Which infuriates her.

Why are they all just *standing* there? Do they not realize that particular alarm signals a certified national state of emergency?

"Umm . . . guys?" Shuri says as she approaches.

The one propped up against the wall with his arms crossed—as though he's watching a particularly boring game of cricket, Shuri thinks—looks in her direction and snaps to attention. "Princess Shuri!" he says, sparking similar posture-perfecting reactions from the other men scattered about. "What . . . uhhhh . . ." He looks around at the others, clearly hoping for some sort of assistance.

None comes.

There are six of them *loitering* around down here while who knows what is happening to the beloved nation they all took an oath to protect with their lives, and they part to give Shuri access to the security room itself.

What she discovers inside makes her want to fire the whole lot of uniformed men posthaste. One guard sits at the central computer barking out erratic orders to four others who are moving around the room flipping different switches and pushing buttons. There's even a guy on his hands and knees poking around beneath the main desk.

"What on earth is going on here?" Shuri says.

The guy in the middle looks over his shoulder at her, then turns back to—whatever it is he's doing. "Princess Shuri!" he says. "What are you doing here, miss?"

Shuri huffs. "I mean you no disrespect, *sir*, but I am of the mind to ask you the same question," she says. "Shouldn't you all be headed to your assigned posts at the border?"

"Huh?" he says, turning to her again, a look of utter bewilderment etched into his bushy eyebrows.

"Your *posts*?" Shuri says more pointedly. "At the *border*."

"OWW!" the one on the floor exclaims as he tries to get out from beneath the desk but fails to clear the edge. He rubs the back of his head as he sits up on his knees. "I don't think she knows, sir," he says to the guard at the desk.

"Oh." And the lead guard turns away from the princess to return to his task. "Balu, try flipping *up* the third switch on the left at the same time you flip *down* the second from the right, and then Idizi will push the button above the third monitor—"

"*What* are you all doing?" Shuri says, throwing her hands in the air this time.

"She definitely doesn't know," comes the voice of a guard who has poked his head in the door.

"What do I not know?!"

Now the head guard sighs. Heavily.

And Shuri instantly feels like exactly what she knows they think she is: a hysterical little girl very much out of her depth.

"It's a false alarm, Your Majesty," he says. "We are trying—as instructed by the king and queen—to turn the thing *off*."

"Huh?" It's out of Shuri's mouth before she can catch it, and she instantly wishes she could take it back—how utterly *silly* she must seem to these men! However, she *needs* more information.

"There is no impending attack or national emergency, dear," the one on the left—Balu—says. "Oy, I forget myself! *Your Majesty*," he corrects with a small bow.

Shuri clenches her jaw to keep from rolling her eyes.

"The alarm was triggered from within," he continues.

Now Shuri's brow furrows. "But that would mean—"

"Someone pulled it," the head guard says impatiently. "Now, if there is nothing else we can do for you, it is imperative that we get back to—"

Shuri shoves past him, taps around on the touchscreen of the control panel, and, when a dialogue box pops up, shifts her hands to the keyboard, types the phrase *Wakanda over Everyone!*, and hits the enter key with more force than is expressly necessary.

The alarm shuts off.

"You're welcome," she says to the guards.

Then she turns on her heel and exits, tapping a Kimoyo bead on her arm to shut the light off in the room, leaving the men in the dark on her way out.

Shuri *plans* to hole up in her quarters, where she can bury her sorrows in a reread of her favorite Advanced Quantum Physics textbook.

In fact, the moment she steps into the space, she makes a beeline for the bookcase, plucks the well-worn tome from the third shelf, and plops herself down in the cushioned nook.

Which is when she notices a different textbook—her

Global Diplomacy one (that she admittedly would like to burn at this moment)—on the floor. Open.

With the pages facedown.

The most cardinal of book sins . . . (Well . . . other than dog-earing.)

It's something Shuri would *never* do.

A chill creeps over her skin as her eyes roam the room. At first glance, the changes are subtle: The digital clock on her bedside table is slightly out of place, and one of the drawers is cracked open. There's a pillow at the foot of the bed that Shuri is certain she left at the head, and the T-shirt she slept in is on the floor instead of hanging off the headboard where she tossed it.

And the light in her dressing chamber is on. Which . . . well, after years of listening to her mother's lectures about not taking solar power for granted, Shuri knows is something *she* isn't responsible for.

Someone was here in her room.

And could very well still be.

Slowly, quietly, Shuri reaches into the secret compartment at the back of her bedside table and pulls out the mini sound cannon she keeps there. While it doesn't seem like much to the naked eye, the princess knows its power.

Then she sneaks across the space to the brightly lit doorway.

"Who's there?" she says, whipping around the corner with the little cannon extended. And while the princess is relieved to see that there's no one inside, she's none too thrilled about the rest of her discovery.

The whole place has been ransacked. There are clothes and shoes scattered about every which way, and what's worse, her miniature lab station is wide open (and she *knows* she didn't leave it that way because she keeps it "hidden" from her mother despite the fact that the queen knows it's there). Shuri rushes over and quickly discovers that in addition to a few broken flasks and vials, there are items *missing*: a sound cannon like the one Shuri is presently holding, a small Panther gauntlet that shoots a purple-toned mini electromagnetic pulse, a pair of CatEyez, and a pair of *very* sharp throwing stars.

The princess can't form a coherent thought, let alone decipher what she's feeling or put together sounds to make words. She turns away from the slaughtered station to do a bit of deep breathing. Collect herself . . .

But then she notices the sheet of paper on the pull-out desk and her mouth goes dry.

It's a list. The phrase *Bright Futures* is scrawled across the top, and beside the number three is a smudge where it's clear someone failed to fully erase the name that was there before—*Princess Shuri of Wakanda*. But scrawled over the botched erase job is a new name. The same one she failed to make out in her dream, but can read clear as ethylene glycol now.

Shuri gasps and snatches the paper up to examine it more closely. And while there's nothing additional to see on *that* sheet, she does unearth something else: a small envelope with her name on it in familiar loopy scrawl.

That's when the princess knows:

K'Marah's gone.

MISSION LOG
(SORT OF ...)

Archived Document
Type: Letter
Format: Handwritten
Date: [unknown]

DEAR SHURI,

I AM SURE THIS LETTER WILL COME
AS A SURPRISE CONSIDERING OUR
MOST RECENT ENCOUNTER. I WAS IN
A NOT-GREAT HEADSPACE WHEN YOU
LAST SAW ME, PARTIALLY DUE TO MY
BEING UNDER THE IMPRESSION THAT
<u>YOU</u> WOULD BE LEAVING <u>ME</u> FOR THE
GARDEN FAIRLY IMMINENTLY. IT
SEEMED THE PERFECT PLACE FOR

YOU, AND SEEING YOUR NAME ON LADY NIRVANA'S LIST OF "BRIGHT FUTURES" REALLY DID A NUMBER ON ME.

SPEAKING OF SAID LIST—AND OF LADY NIRVANA (THAT'S WHAT THE "N" IS FOR, BY THE WAY)—SHORTLY AFTER YOU LEFT MY HOUSE YESTERDAY, I RECEIVED A MESSAGE ON MY KIMOYO CARD INFORMING ME THAT I, IN FACT, HAD BEEN CHOSEN AS THE "NEXT RECRUIT FOR PLANTING IN THE GARDEN." DON'T TAKE THIS THE WRONG WAY, BUT DURING THE BRIEF VIDEO CHAT I HAD WITH LADY NIRVANA (WHO IS QUITE PRETTY AND STYLISH, BY THE WAY!), SHE TOLD ME THAT WHILE THEY INITIALLY WERE THINKING ABOUT INVITING YOU TO JOIN THEIR RANKS (I WAS RIGHT ABOUT THAT PART, AS YOU CAN SEE), AFTER FURTHER CONSIDERATION, IT WAS DECIDED THAT I WOULD BE THE BETTER CHOICE. "WE HAVE MANY INVENTORS AND TECHNOLOGICAL SAVANTS, BUT NO RECRUITS WHO ARE SKILLED IN TACTICAL STRATEGY

AND HAND-TO-HAND COMBAT," SHE
SAID.

I HAVEN'T TOLD YOU THIS BECAUSE I
DIDN'T WANT YOU TRYING TO *FIX*
ANYTHING ON MY BEHALF, BUT A FEW
WEEKS AGO, I GOT INTO SOME
TROUBLE WITH OKOYE OVER
SOMETHING I GENUINELY DIDN'T DO.
IN A NUTSHELL, THE GENERAL IS
UNDER THE IMPRESSION THAT I WAS
THE ONE WHO TOLD YOU ABOUT THAT
CONCLAVE YOUR BROTHER IS
ATTENDING. I HAVE NO IDEA WHERE
SHE GOT THAT IDEA BUT IT HAS
CAUSED HER TO WATCH ME MORE
CLOSELY AND SHARE LESS
INFORMATION. IN OTHER WORDS, DORA
TRAINING ISN'T AS . . . LIFE-GIVING,
AS YOU WOULD SAY, AS IT USED TO BE.

RECEIVING THAT MESSAGE AND CALL
MADE ME FEEL LIKE I WAS GETTING
A CHANCE AT SOMETHING NEW. IN
THE SPIRIT OF HONESTY HERE, I
WILL CONFESS TO YOU THAT WHILE
I DEFINITELY ENJOY BEING YOUR

BEST FRIEND, SEEING YOUR NAME ON THAT LIST, ESPECIALLY AFTER MY FALSE-ACCUSATION INCIDENT, REALLY MADE ME FEEL . . . WELL, NOT VERY GOOD ABOUT MYSELF AND MY "PLACE," IF YOU WILL, IN WAKANDA.

THERE IS JUST SO MUCH PRESSURE AND SO MANY EXPECTATIONS, AS I'M SURE YOU KNOW. IT'S JUST . . . THINGS ARE DIFFERENT FOR ME THAN THEY ARE FOR YOU. YOU'RE THE PRINCESS. IN MANY WAYS, YOU CAN DO NO WRONG. IF YOU MESS UP, PEOPLE WILL COVER FOR YOU. I WILL COVER FOR YOU EVEN. IF I MESS UP, I BRING SHAME UPON THE DORA MILAJE AND MY ENTIRE FAMILY. BOTH OF WHICH ARE SUBJECTED TO YOU AND YOURS.

I DON'T MEAN FOR ANY OF THIS TO SOUND PERSONAL, I JUST . . . WELL, RECEIVING THAT INVITATION TO THE GARDEN DID A LOT FOR ME. I WOULDN'T HAVE ADMITTED IT BEFORE BECAUSE I JUST KNEW THERE WAS ZERO CHANCE OF A GIRL LIKE ME

GETTING INVITED TO A PLACE LIKE
THE GARDEN—MY "SMARTS" ARE MORE
"STREET" THAN "BOOK," AS THEY SAY
IN AMERICA. BUT BEING IN THAT
FACILITY WAS . . . I MEAN, YOU WERE
THERE. YOU KNOW HOW AMAZING IT
WAS. EVER SINCE WE GOT BACK, I'VE
FELT THIS . . . LOSS.

ANYWAY. THIS IS GETTING LONG.

WHAT YOU SHOULD KNOW: BY THE
TIME YOU READ THIS, I WILL BE
GONE. I TRIGGERED THE EMERGENCY
ALERT. (SORRY. IT WAS THE ONLY
BIG-ENOUGH DIVERSION I COULD
THINK OF FOR GETTING TO MY
RENDEZVOUS POINT WITH LADY
NIRVANA UNNOTICED.) ALSO, I TOOK A
FEW OF YOUR GADGETY THINGS. I'D
LOVE TO SAY "BORROWED," BUT I'M NOT
SURE I'LL EVER BE ABLE TO GET
THEM BACK TO YOU. AGAIN: SORRY.

LASTLY, IF YOU WIND UP GOING TO
THAT CONCLAVE THING I WAS
ACCUSED OF TELLING YOU ABOUT, I'LL
LIKELY SEE YOU THERE.

THAT'S THE COOLEST PART OF ALL
THIS: LADY NIRVANA HAS A PLAN TO
MAKE THE WORLD A MORE WELCOMING
PLACE FOR YOUNG GIRLS. NO MORE
LIFE ON THE FRINGES! PHASE ONE OF
HER PLAN WILL KICK OFF AT THAT
CONCLAVE. WHO KNOWS: PERHAPS
YOU'LL BE SO IMPRESSED WITH WHAT
WE'RE DOING, YOU'LL DECIDE TO LEAVE
WITH US INSTEAD OF RETURNING TO
WAKANDA WITH YOUR BROTHER.

LASTLY, I WOULD GREATLY APPRECIATE
IT IF YOU DIDN'T TELL MY MOTHER OR
GRANDMOTHER ANYTHING. MOTHER IS
UNDER THE IMPRESSION THAT I AM
PARTICIPATING IN SOME EXTENDED
DORA MILAJE TRAINING AND WILL BE
GONE FOR AT LEAST A WEEK. I'LL
FIGURE SOMETHING OUT BEYOND THAT.

YOU REALLY HAVE BEEN AN
EXCELLENT FRIEND (FOR THE MOST
PART). I'LL MISS YOU.

SINCERELY,

K'MARAH

18
DESPERATE TIMES

This is all my fault.

The words ring over and over in Shuri's head as she bolts from her quarters and heads to the roof. Without waiting for permission or an escort, she summons the *Predator* and heads straight for the lab. "Hey, S.H.U.R.I., call Riri Williams," she says as the sleek black vessel shoots off in the direction of the sacred mound.

This is all my fault.

The puzzle pieces slide together in Shuri's mind, and she shakes her head. *She* is the reason K'Marah got into trouble. *She* told her mother and T'Challa that K'Marah had spilled the beans about the conclave. She lied.

And look what has happened.

"Hello?" comes a shockingly gruff voice through the *Predator*'s speakers.

"Uhhh . . . hello? May I . . . speak to Riri?"

"This *is* Riri." The person groans.

"Oh. Umm, this is Princess Shuri. Of Wakanda—"

"I *know* who you are, Shuri. Caller ID. Which is surely a thing there, too. What do you *want*, is the question. It's four in the morning."

"Oh my goodness," Shuri says, smacking her forehead. The *Predator*'s hangar yawns wide in front of her. "I didn't think of the time difference. I'm so sorry."

"It's fine, it's fine. What's up?"

As the travel vessel touches down, Shuri begins to relay the information she should've been sharing with Riri all along: that there was a ping on Pilar Bautista's name the moment Shuri entered it into the P.R.O.W.L. network. That it gave her a location. That said location was also written on an invitation—in French—that a friend of Shuri's friend received. That Shuri and Shuri's friend visited said location and discovered a veritable STEM wonderland that was admittedly a bit creepy. That while *inside* the STEM wonderland, Shuri not only saw, but spoke to, Riri's friend Cici. (Riri stops her here. "You *TALKED* to Cici and didn't tell me??" she shouts, fully awake now, apparently.)

The narrow escape—and Pilar sighting. The hole in Shuri's memory regarding the trip back. The bizarre dreams and dizzying replay of that music in Shuri's mind. The latest ping and K'Marah not caring about it.

"It was about her," Riri says when Shuri finishes reading the transcript aloud.

"Huh?"

"That transcript. They must've been talking about your friend."

"What do you mean?"

"Think about it. It came from Kampala, Uganda, right? Which I believe you once told me is the city where *your* friend met her *French* friend who had gone missing, yeah? And they said the lead *came* from your friend's French friend. And there was something about combat and then mention of a distance— geography isn't my strongest suit, especially with the whole miles versus kilometers thing, but I do believe your country is probably in the range she mentioned regarding distance and direction from Kampala."

"Huh" is all Shuri can manage.

"But the sealer of the deal for me was the mention

of the words *two recruits, instead,* and *too high-profile*. Especially taken in tandem with that bizarre dream you were having about that list and your name disappearing. And you said that the new name that appears in the dream turned out to be hers?"

Now Shuri feels like an imbecile. Why didn't she see it before? She'd even held the actual list in her hand with the change on it.

"We have to save her," Shuri says, shifting the call to her Kimoyo card and heading into the center lab station so she can access the P.R.O.W.L.

"*Them*," Riri replies.

"Yes. *Them*. ALL of them. Because while I don't know *exactly* what this 'Lady Nirvana' has planned, I certainly don't feel particularly good about it."

Over the next hour and thirty minutes, Shuri and Riri work in tandem gathering intel and formulating a plan.

According to the S.H.I.E.L.D. file Riri manages to infiltrate, "Nirvana" is the suspected *new* alias of a scientific genius and criminal mastermind named Tilda Johnson—formerly known as Nightshade. ("What is it with the poisonous-plant villain pseudonyms?" Shuri wonders aloud, and then has to tell Riri about Henbane and the whole heart-shaped herb drama from a few months back.)

"If these records are telling it right," Riri says as Shuri tries (again) to hack the Garden's network, "this Nightshade/Nirvana lady isn't anybody to sneeze at."

"I'll pretend I know what that means," Shuri replies.

"Means she's a fairly formidable adversary. She's apparently had run-ins with the likes of Captain America and the Falcon—those are Super Heroes on this side of the pond, and big-deal ones at that. Did you say something about this Garden place having a certain smell?"

ACCESS DENIED flashes in bright red on Shuri's screen as another hack attempt fails. "Mm-hmm," she says absentmindedly.

"It might be one of her control mechanisms."

That gets Shuri's attention. "Huh?"

"Says here that she incapacitated those heroes I mentioned utilizing some sort of mind-warping chemicals that are delivered to the central nervous system through the olfactory glands."

This gives Shuri pause . . . and a shiver. It smelled so *good* inside the Garden. Could a fragrance that pleasant really be used for something as insidious as mind control? "That is vaguely terrifying."

"Vaguely?"

"I am trying to, ah, 'keep my head in the game,' as I believe you say over there."

"Got it. Well, speaking of your head, you should definitely protect your nose and mouth to keep from inhaling the air in the Garden when you return there. Have you finished formulating your plan?"

"Ummm . . ." No. Shuri hasn't. She's been too busy trying to break into the place virtually.

"Okay, *I* will take over Operation Infiltration so *you* can decide how you want to handle getting back to Ethiopia."

"Well, getting *there* is the easy part," Shuri replies. "My transport vessel will cover the distance in no time. It's getting *out*—of both Wakanda AND the Garden—that will prove . . . tricky."

"Okayyyy . . ." Riri says. "Not that it matters, but aren't you, like . . . kind of a big deal? Yeah, you're young, but can't you just order somebody to cover for you or something?"

"Tuh." *If only*, Shuri thinks. "Not sure how much you gathered about me or my homeland the first time you went poking around in my files, but what you are suggesting is not the best idea."

While Shuri is inclined to just pop into the *Predator* and make a run for it—she's obviously done it before— leaving without *any* adults knowing feels . . . not right. Especially considering the heightened state of awareness everyone is sure to still be in after that alarm . . .

However, the current chaos in the city would also serve as a good cover for her departure.

She could call Nakia. Fill her in and ask for her assistance. In truth, not having to go it alone would be nice . . .

But . . . what all does the Dora Milaje oath entail? Is Nakia bound to report all matters of national security—because surely a princess departing a nation without her mother's knowledge is a matter of national security—to General Okoye?

Shuri could tell the clothier. Ask him to cover for her. It is *his* niece the princess is going after . . .

But what if he's angry over Shuri's inability to break through to K'Marah like he asked her to? What if . . . he feels that K'Marah's disappearance is Shuri's fault? She cannot deny the possibility that upon hearing that his beloved niece is no longer in Wakanda, he will immediately alert *all* the mothers—Shuri's, K'Marah's, and his own: the mining tribe's proverbial overlord, Eldress Umbusi.

THAT would be a disaster of proportions more epic than the state-of-emergency alarms signaling a true state of emergency.

The bracelet on Shuri's right wrist vibrates and illuminates with an incoming call.

General Okoye. (*Oh boy.*)

"Riri, I need to put you on hold for just one moment, okay?"

"Will there be cheesy music?" the American girl replies.

"*Cheese* music? What on earth is that?"

"Never mind. Handle your business, I'll be here."

After straightening her braids, Shuri takes the call in hologram-mode. She wants the general to *see* her so there's no suspicion of impending foul play. "Hello, General!" Shuri says, chipper as ever, when she answers.

"Princess! Thank Bast. You are safe?"

"I am," Shuri replies. "I came to my lab to escape some of the mayhem. The palace guards told me the alarm was false?"

"Yes. It was. But . . ." Okoye's gaze darts about. "One moment, please, Your Majesty. I need to get somewhere more private."

Shuri's stomach loop-the-loops. "Okay," she says, trying to keep her pulse in check.

After a few seconds, Okoye's image reemerges. It's much quieter in the background now. "Shuri? Are you still there?"

"Yes, General."

"Are you alone?"

What to say to that? Should she pretend K'Marah is

with her? How did this get so complicated so quickly?

"I am alone, yes," Shuri says.

Okoye sighs. "That is most unfortunate," she says.

"What? Why?"

Now Okoye's face goes slack at the edges. As though her typically stern self just *can't even*, as K'Marah would say. "I think something has happened to K'Marah, Shuri. She's been acting so strangely these past two weeks, and I just received a phone call from her mother asking about some training intensive K'Marah said she'd be attending for the next five days. I didn't blow her cover because I *hoped* the alibi was for something involving *you*. But knowing she's not with you . . . I am very worried, Shuri."

And there it is: an opening. It's with the last person on earth Shuri would've expected (besides her mother, that is . . .), which could either be a blessing in disguise from Bast herself, or a freshly paved path to being "grounded" indefinitely.

Shuri sure hopes it's the former. What's that phrase? Desperate times call for desperate measures?

She takes Riri off hold to let her know she'll call her back. And then Shuri tells Okoye everything.

19

. . . GIRLS

Within an hour, the princess and the general are flying over the neighboring nation of Mohannda and on the verge of crossing into Ethiopia. Neither has said very much since Okoye boarded the *Predator* at their chosen point of contact in the baobab field. And while Shuri can only speculate about the reasons for the general's silence, her own is a function of how bizarre it is to have her brother *and* mother's right-hand woman . . . sitting to her right.

Shuri knows Okoye is really here for K'Marah's sake. The general admitted to feeling quite guilty over her refusal to believe the Dora-in-training really *hadn't* told Shuri about the conclave. "She'd never lied before," Okoye said over their Kimoyo call. "How could I have doubted her character so easily? I am so ashamed." Shuri's hope is that the apology Okoye said she would issue the moment she *sees* K'Marah (and of course Shuri will issue one of her own) will be enough to help K'Marah see how cherished—and needed— she is in Wakanda.

Shuri sneaks a peek at the older woman. Despite the sharp lines and angles of her Dora Milaje garb, General Okoye is endlessly elegant. Especially in comparison with the high-tech but utilitarian interior of the *Predator*. Her presence is almost too much for Shuri to fathom.

She'd been surprised when Okoye said she'd join Shuri on the trip back to the Garden. For as long as Shuri can remember, she's never seen Okoye leave T'Challa's side. (Or even Baba's before him.) "You, uhhh . . . won't get into any trouble for leaving your post, right?" Shuri says sheepishly.

Now Okoye laughs. "I can assure you, Princess: Everyone will survive a few hours without me."

They lapse back into silence for a beat, and then:

"Quite the vessel you have here, Princess," Okoye suddenly says, looking around at the control panel.

"Ah. Umm . . . thank you, General."

"I'm guessing 'downtime' isn't really a *thing* for you these days, but if you happen to get particularly bored in the near future, feel free to build one of these for *me*."

At this, Shuri laughs. And relaxes a bit.

"Will you show me the schematic of this place we're going?" Okoye continues.

"Oh yes. My apologies, General."

As Shuri projects the re-rendered image from her Kimoyo card into the air, Okoye intakes a breath. "Yes," she says. "Definitely would like one of these." She takes her index finger and taps the edge of the three-dimensional image. It rotates and zooms in. "Marvelous," she whispers.

"The plan is for me to enter the same way I did before," Shuri says, breaking the older woman's trance (and feeling a smidge bad about it, but it's time to get down to business). "My hope is that K'Marah hasn't lost her *whole* mind and has stayed mum about our previous invisible visit. That way, they—again, *hopefully*—won't have changed the passwords, and the mechanism for getting inside will be the same."

A ringing sound pierces the pressurized air, and the general startles. Which makes Shuri chuckle under her breath. She answers the incoming call. "Hello?"

"Are you close?" says a girl's voice.

Shuri rolls her eyes. "Hello to you, too, Riri."

"Oh. Sorry. Hi. Are you close?"

"We're getting there. General, this is Riri Williams," Shuri says to Okoye. "She's the girl in Chicago I mentioned who will be helping out on the digital front."

"Hello, Riri," Okoye says with a smile.

"Wait. Did you say *general*?" comes Riri's reply. "Wow. Seems extreme to bring along military personnel, but hey: You do you."

Okoye chuckles. "I like this one."

"Riri, any additional headway in cracking the Garden's network?" Shuri asks.

"I've gotten *very* close a couple of times, but just when I think I've gotten through the final firewall, this taunting message from some entity who calls itself Kitty Pryde pops up and says, 'Uh-uh-uh! No peeking!' It's infuriating."

"Okay, well, once I'm in, my Kimoyo card should automatically connect, and you should hopefully be able to pick up the signal. I'll head straight for the Hive and plant a chip in their mainframe. Which *should* give you complete access. You can shut down whatever systems are keeping the place hidden *and* filling the air with that fragrance, and the girls will snap out of it."

Shuri then turns to Okoye. "Once that happens, I'll send you a Kimoyo alert that sounds like this . . ." Shuri taps a bead on her bracelet, and a three-tone chime rings out.

"Noted," Okoye says with a nod. (*Is the general* really *here right now??* Shuri thinks.)

"When you hear it, you can call T'Challa and have him send the Pouncer Jets. They'll get here fast and have the space necessary to transport at least fifty girls each. I still don't know exactly how many there are inside."

"At least seventy-five of the disappearances I've been tracking are connected to this," Riri says.

"Wow." Okoye's eyes narrow. "And this woman's plan is to do precisely *what* with the captures?"

"Well, based on the background of who we *think* she is, she'll do what every extra-*basic* villain does," Riri replies.

"Try to take over the world," from Shuri. Who shivers. Because while she doesn't know this Lady Nirvana woman, she does know a bad feeling when she has one. *You must trust your instincts, Panther Cub,* she can hear Kocha M'Shindi saying in her head.

"You're *sure* I don't need to go in with you, Princess?" the general says, apparently unable to resist *her* (protective) instincts.

"I'm sure," Shuri says. "If something goes down, I need you outside ready to call for backup . . . Not that I think anything will go down," she adds at the sight of Okoye's conflicted face.

The general sighs. And relents. "Well," she says, "here's hoping everything goes according to plan."

Shuri just nods and increases the *Predator*'s speed. Then she and Riri speak simultaneously: "Couldn't've said it better myself."

Things do go according to plan.

At first.

After testing her new in-suit comm system—and making sure Okoye can't hear her talking outside it (check)—Shuri completes an infrared scan of the crystalized salt terrain to locate the Garden so that she can land the Invisi-moded *Predator* near one of the emergency exits. Then she goes to the spot where the door is, and gets herself inside as before.

This time when the elevator door begins to open on the experimentation floor, Shuri's already facing that way. Ready to go. There's a decent amount of foot traffic in the hall before her, but she knows she has to move fast, so she slips out before the panel has opened all the way.

Good thing, too. The moment one of the girls

notices—Britt, if Shuri remembers correctly—she halts and shouts, "Nobody move!" then proceeds to walk *into* the elevator and do a full sweep with her arms outstretched in front of her.

"Uhh . . . Britt? Are you okay?"

"I'm fine, I just—"

"Please step out of the elevator."

Shuri stifles a laugh as she heads up the hallway, a task that is much easier now that no one is moving.

"Shuri! I'm in! Well . . . partially," Riri's voice says (loudly) into Shuri's ear.

"Okay. You don't need to yell, though?"

"Sorry," Riri says. "Got excited. I secured access to that virtual map thing with all the moving dots on it, so now you won't be totally blind in there. Man, this woman sure is obsessed with hexagons, huh? After the second bend, hang a right into the engineering wing. There are two dots—I mean *girls*—approaching the exit, so you should be able to go in as they leave."

"Got it."

"And more good news: The Hive is empty."

Shuri's heart lifts. This is going better than she hoped.

"I don't see a computer mainframe in there on *this* map . . . but I don't see one anywhere else, either, so there's that."

"Okay."

"There are three different entry doors to the Hive. I'll guide you around to the one that has the fewest girls close by. It's at the back end of the mathematics sector."

"Got it." Shuri crosses the engineering space, doing her best not to get distracted by the myriad activities going on within it. There's a trio of girls building some sort of machine, another set creating a model of a suspension bridge from magnetic tiles, and a pair standing by a 3-D printer—all in orange.

Shuri clenches her jaw: They all look to be having the times of their lives.

"Man, I gotta say: If that place is as cool as it looks from this map, I can see why none of the girls have gone home," Riri says (unhelpfully) into Shuri's ear. "You protected your nose so you won't inhale the air, right?"

At this, Shuri sighs. She doesn't *mean* to. It's just . . . well, she *liked* how good this place felt the first time she visited. And she misses that feeling.

"Whoa," Riri suddenly says.

"What?" Shuri's heart rate kicks up. "Did something happen?"

"Uhhh . . . not yet? But something will if we fail this mission. With you connected to the network,

I was able to crack into a file I'm sure Lady N wouldn't want *anyone* to see."

A drone zips over Shuri's head, and she has to duck. "What's in it?"

"Her . . . plans. I won't go into detail because you need to stay focused. But the long and short of it is that she has zero intention of ever allowing these girls to return to their families. In super-basic-villain fashion, she's creating an army."

There is definitely some sort of mind-control juice in the air. "To what end, though?"

"Pause. You're approaching the math-and-technology sector now, which wraps around the Hive." Shuri notices that as she gets closer to said sector, the jumpsuits shift from orange to red. "At the dead end, bank right, and then left. The room is shaped like a—"

"Hexagon, I know," Shuri says, following the directions. Most of the girls she passes are so immersed in their respective work, Shuri doubts they'd notice her even if she strutted through in a neon pink leotard with a feathered crown singing "I Will Survive" at the top of her lungs. "Can we get back to Lady N's plans?"

"Seems to be your classic *I was scorned and now I hate everyone* vendetta. There's a journal entry where she mentions the pain of being sidelined for men even though she was the better candidate for like jobs and stuff."

Shuri tries to ignore the pinch in her chest.

"Honestly, her reason for being low-key evil isn't super far-fetched. The world *isn't* super kind to nerd girls like us. But despite being all about girl power myself, I personally can't rock with kidnapping and brainwashing people."

"Fair point," Shuri says.

"There should be a Hive entrance in a wall to your left."

Shuri sees it . . . but also sees the number pad where a passcode has to be entered.

"Drat!" Shuri says. "The door is code-protected."

"Oh," Riri replies. "Probably should've expected that."

"You didn't happen to get control of the doors yet, did you?"

"Nope."

With a huff, Shuri looks around. She has ONE chance to get this right. Her eyes land on a light-brown-skinned girl, bent over a notebook and scribbling furiously. Shuri steps closer and looks over the girl's shoulder. The most complex math problem the princess has ever seen unfurls across the page.

A memory pops into Shuri's head: K'Marah

walking over to Shuri's digital safe, inputting the correct passcode, and having her way with Shuri's stash of sweets. "How did you do that?" the princess had asked. And K'Marah shrugged. "You flat-out told me the password while working on one of your experiments. I asked, and you answered."

Shuri swallows nervously, then presses the button she added to the suit's right wrist so that her silencer will turn off temporarily. She leans down near the girl's ear. "Hey, sorry to interrupt, but I forgot the passcode to the Hive—"

"Nine-three-seven-eight-six," the girl says without breaking her concentration.

Quick as she can, Shuri zips back to the door, and inputs the numbers.

When the door parts down the center, she exhales.

And then she slips inside.

Which is when everything begins to go terribly wrong. Because as soon as the door has shut behind Shuri, she can hear a strange buzzing sound just ahead. She's in a short passageway with a frosted glass door at the opposite end. There's a dark shape beyond it, but Shuri can't make it out. "Riri? You picking up on that noise?"

"Vaguely," the other girl says in Shuri's ear. "It's probably just the hum of all the fans in the mainframe.

I'm sure you know how intense supercomputers can be. Go ahead and try to plant the chip before someone comes."

"Fine," Shuri says, swallowing down her sense of foreboding. "The coast is clear?"

"As rubbing alcohol."

Pulling the chip from the flapped breast pocket she added to the suit, Shuri shoves through the second door.

And stops dead in her tracks. Because there at the center of the Hive is the largest *literal* hive the princess has ever seen: Sheets of honeycomb hang from the paneled ceiling like swaths of dripping paint, each one completely covered in honeybees. Who have definitely come to realize there's an intruder and gotten louder. "Oh my GODS!" Shuri says, feeling behind her for the door handle so she can go out the same way she came in.

Except there isn't one.

"Riri, how do I get out of here? This 'hive' is full of *bees* that *sting* when agitated, and I am ONE HUNDRED percent sure they're agitated!"

"Oh WOW! Definitely didn't see *that* com—"

"RIRI!"

"Okay, okay! I'm looking!"

Shuri begins to slide to the right along the wall. Yes, her suit can withstand the type of radiation levels that cause genetic mutations, but will the material hold up if attacked by the stingers of thousands of honeybees?

She certainly doesn't want to find out.

"Move to the left!" Riri says. (Of *course* the princess went the wrong way. Of COURSE!) "After you feel yourself shift over the second angle in the hexagon, there will be a door in the center of the wall. There's a padlock symbol over it on this digital schematic just like there was over the door you used to enter, so I'm guessing—hoping, really—there's a keypad where you'll enter the same code. It leads to a corridor with an exit that'll spit you out at the back of the VR space."

"Okay," Shuri says, whispering now.

"We need to get you outta there. Regroup. This is proving more difficult than I anticipated."

"YEP!" Shuri says, inching closer as the bees whip about in front of her. One lands on the back of her (thankfully gloved) hand, and she freezes.

It flies away, Bast be praised.

"Just so you know: There are a *lot* of girls congregated in the space you have to go through. I'm sure the ones who aren't immersed in whatever they're doing will notice when the door opens, so just move fast. Head back to the main hallway—"

"And go straight across and down the hall to the emergency exit on the biology wing—"

"No, actually," Riri says. "That will set off an alarm. Which we don't need."

"Umm . . . okay?"

"There's an additional exit to the right of the elevator that will put you in a stairwell. It connects to the main entry room. That's the way you'll go."

Shuri has reached the keypad, and after a deep breath, she spins around, punches in the code, and the moment the door hisses open, she goes through it and shoves it shut behind her as fast as she can. Two rogue bees manage to slip through, but she can't think about that right now.

"All right, I'm approaching the second door."

"Okay. There's a trio of girls standing not too far beyond it, so be careful."

"Noted."

Shuri readies herself to make a break for it, thankful to see what looks like a sensor above the door that will cause it to open automatically. Then she steps forward.

The wall parts, and the bees slip out (oops), but Shuri is on the move.

Until she's not.

Because the sight of the three girls Riri mentioned

makes Shuri feel as if she's slammed into a brick wall. There are two in orange and one in gray, all examining what looks like a prosthetic leg and chattering away in French.

Which instantly stops when they notice the open door.

The girl in gray's eyes widen and dart around. As if she knows something's afoot.

Shuri's mouth opens and closes, but no sound comes out. Then she locks eyes with the girl (or so it seems).

And Shuri is absolutely certain the girl knows that Shuri is there.

It's K'Marah.

20

NIGHTSHADE

And then someone screams.

"BEEEE!"

"Oh my gosh, *where*?!"

"We have to get OUT of here!"

"Why does Lady N even *keep* those things?"

"Well, she mentioned the creation of a paralysis serum made from the toxin in a honeybee's venom sac—"

"It was rhetorical, Celeste!"

As the fleeing frenzy catches on, the whole room is thrown into chaos. Different girls continue to voice their complaints as they duck and dodge and swipe at the air in their rush toward the exit into the main hallway.

It serves as both blessing and curse.

On the one hand, if the room empties out, it'll be easy for Shuri to walk through unnoticed.

On the other: Now there's a clump of girls trying to get into the hall. Thereby blocking her way to freedom.

"Shuri, what's happening?" Riri says. "All the floating dots in the room have converged."

"Yep," Shuri replies. "A couple of bees got out of the hive, and everyone panicked and is trying to exit."

"Ah."

"So . . . plan B?"

"I mean, there really isn't one. Stay close to the crowd, I guess, and we'll hope that if you accidentally bump somebody, it'll be ignored in the shuffle."

Shuri reluctantly complies, getting as close as she can to the group—there are maybe twenty-five girls— and as they move, the princess's gaze hooks onto the back of K'Marah's head and won't let go.

How can Shuri reach her friend? Will she be able to get the young Dora trainee to see sense? Because, by Bast, K'Marah *is* still going to be to Shuri what Okoye is to T'Challa. The princess won't have it any other way.

How will Shuri get her friend's head cleared of the

hypnotic gas she's inhaled? Based on how clearheaded Shuri is when *not* breathing the air, the princess is now sure—

"WHO RUN THE WORLD?"

Everyone freezes.

Shuri curses under her breath and backs away from the others as she tries to silence her blaring Kimoyo card within her pocket.

K'Marah whips around.

"What was that?" someone else says, all desire to escape the room evidently forgotten.

"WHO RUN THE WORLD?"

"What's that awful stench?" another girl says, sniffing at the air.

Shuri fumbles with the device—blasted *gloves*—unable to remove it: Music coming from seemingly nowhere is a smidge different from a smartphone-style device floating in midair.

"Shuri, what's going on?"

"It would appear that my mother is calling," the princess hisses. "I'm trying to turn it off—"

All the girls gasp.

"Oh boy," K'Marah says, looking at Shuri.

Who looks down. And instead of seeing nothing, sees a torso, legs, and feet clad in neon purple polyethylene.

The Kimoyo card stops ringing. (Because of *course* it does.)

Nobody speaks. Shuri doesn't even breathe.

The girls do, though. She knows because some of their faces change. "Sheesh, does it reek in here, or is it just me?" one girl says, waving her hand in front of her nose.

"Definitely *not* just you." This girl is pinching *her* nose shut.

"It *does* stink," a third girl says. Shuri's eyes widen with recognition: Xiang Yeh. A Chinese Jamaican girl Shuri's age known for her work using virtual reality to create new neurological connections in people who have suffered traumatic brain injuries. The princess is in awe just looking at her.

And Xiang is staring right back. "But it certainly didn't stink a minute ago."

The girls begin to murmur to one another, and Xiang runs her eyes over the walls and ceiling before fixing them on Shuri again . . . and then coming toward her.

The princess couldn't move if her life depended on it.

"Hey! It's starting to smell better!" says a girl with big, curly hair.

More of them inhale.

And it might be a trick of the light, but Shuri could swear she sees some of their eyes glaze over as they do.

"Wait, why is there someone in a hazmat suit in the engineering wing?"

"Yeah . . . who's she?"

"Hold on a sec," Xiang says, putting a hand up to silence the girls behind her.

To Shuri's shock, they all comply.

Now Xiang is right in front of her. Shuri wishes the suit had a "vaporization" option.

But then the other girl, who is a similar height and build as the princess, says something Shuri *isn't* expecting:

"Will you turn that song back on?"

Shuri opens her mouth to reply, but thinks better of it. "Shuri?" comes Riri's voice in her ear. "Are you all right?"

Without a word, Shuri removes a glove and swipes at the screen of her device. The song comes pouring out again—from the top this time—and she watches in amazement as the girls' expressions shift from that bizarrely blissed-out state to confusion. With slack jaws and furrowed brows, they glance at one another, then begin to look around.

"What even *is* this place?" one of them says.

"And what are we doing here?"

"Why does it smell like that?"

"I think there's something wrong," Xiang says, looking over her shoulder at her friends.

"Not to sound like a little kid," comes the voice of a girl with an Australian accent, "but I sort of want me mum."

Xiang turns back to Shuri as the song continues to blare. "Who exactly are—"

But that's all Shuri hears. Because at that moment she feels a tingle behind her left ear, and instinctively leans to the right. Something whizzes past her neck from behind, embedding itself in Xiang's shoulder.

Shuri and Xiang look down at it simultaneously—some sort of dart—before Xiang's limbs go slack and she collapses.

"Oh, *mon dieu*!" says one of the French cousins beside K'Marah.

Shuri whirls around just as a brown-skinned woman (with kind of an epic Mohawk) levels the dart gun she's holding to fire another shot at the princess of Wakanda.

"Shuri, I think Lady N might be behind you!" Riri says.

"Oh, *really*, now?"

"Ah, so you already knew. Great! My work here is done!"

Shuri dodges another dart and hears the *fwump* of another girl genius going down. Then someone cries, "Why is Lady N shooting tranq-darts at us?"

Shuri pushes the button on her wrist again to turn her silencer off. "You girls are in danger," she says aloud, squeezing her remaining gloved hand into a fist to power up the photon blaster she embedded in the palm. "This woman does not have your best interests at heart—"

Another dart whizzes by.

"Don't listen to this *intruder*," Lady N (more like "Lady N-O") says to the group. "She is no one. You are my protégés. The world's best and brightest. And I have a grand purpose for you."

"And what *is* that purpose?" Shuri says, hoping to keep the woman talking. The song is still playing, which means the girls' minds *should* be clear enough for the truth about Lady N's grand plans to ring through whatever crap she's about to feed them.

"These girls have more intelligence in their pinkie fingers than the collective sum in the heads of all the world's male leaders. *I* have more intelligence than ninety-seven percent of the *men* who were chosen or promoted in my stead. I will not permit that to be the case for them."

"Sounds legit to me," a girl in red says.

This certainly isn't going the way Shuri anticipated . . .

Good thing her blaster is ready.

"Now, as for this interloper . . ." The woman fires a final shot, and once Shuri rebounds from dodging it, she shoves her hand forward, palm out. The burst of purple light catches the woman in the right shoulder, and her arm goes limp.

"You need to let these girls go, Nightshade—"

"It's *Nirvana*." And the woman—who isn't *that* much bigger than Shuri, but still—lunges at the princess.

After an incredibly nimble kick-fake that Shuri moves to dodge, the woman swings out with the arm that *should* still be temporarily paralyzed . . . Which catches Shuri off guard.

"What the . . . ?" the princess says, leaning back just in time and barely dodging the blow to the face. She stumbles backward, and the woman kicks out. The princess catches her foot and *twists* just like M'Shindi taught her, but instead of the woman flipping wildly and landing incapacitated on her side, she manages to use the force of Shuri's defensive move to increase her own momentum. Her *other* foot flies around and pegs Shuri in her unguarded side. The princess goes down.

"You should show some respect, girl," Nightshade/Nirvana/*whatever* says, standing over her.

Shuri fires off another photon blast from the floor, and it hits the woman in the hip. She staggers as her leg goes numb . . . but then quickly recovers.

"Riri, how is she doing that?" Shuri says, scrambling back to her feet and getting as far out of the woman's reach as possible. Her Kimoyo card has fallen out of her pocket. "Those blasts should render her limbs useless for a *minimum* of five minutes!"

"I'm looking, I'm looking!" Riri says.

The woman smiles, pulling on a pair of gloves as she approaches Shuri, who is struggling to find her nerve. She can still hear the spell-cracking girl-power song playing, but it's nearing the end.

"You just don't get it, sweetheart," Nirvana says. "I know everything about you. All those *gifts* you have. Wasting away in service to your thickheaded, talentless hack of a brother? You're on the wrong side, dear."

Shuri creeps backward as Lady N advances.

"Aha!" Riri says into Shuri's ear. "There's a report here that says she's like a super genius in both genetics and biochemistry and is known for creating chemical cocktails that can alter human physiology at the cellular level. She probably drinks some sort of self-healing serum in place of a daily multivitamin or something. And apparently once created an army of . . . werewolves?"

"How delightful," Shuri grumbles.

"Just watch out for her hands. There's something here about gloves that can eat through the densest materials on Earth. She's, like . . . a really bomb inventor."

"A *bomb* inventor?"

"That's 'bomb' as in 'cool,'" Riri says.

The song ends. (*Why* hadn't she thought to put it on repeat?)

"We want the same things, you and I," the woman continues.

Shuri is officially against a wall now. Nowhere else to go.

"Aren't you sick of being sidelined, Princess? You are *brilliant*. And so are they." She gestures to the clump of girls, who all look dazed. Some of them shake their heads and look around, and Shuri can tell the toxin in the air is overtaking them again.

And with the silencer in her helmet turned off, Shuri can now hear the Garden music. Which she realizes must be used in tandem with the fragrance to keep the girls subdued.

"She really is a genius," Shuri mumbles as her head goes fuzzy.

"Shuri? What's going on?" Riri shouts into her ear. "Do I need to signal your general now?"

"Come, Princess," Lady N says.

She's so pretty. And so nice. She'll never overlook me . . . The thoughts float through Shuri's head like oil atop water.

"Join us," Lady N continues. "*We* should be ruling this world. You and I and the others. *We* have the smarts to end all wars. *We* can cure the diseases. *We* have the brains to create the tech that will make the world better. *We* can control *everything*, my sweet."

She places her hands on Shuri's shoulders. There's a sizzling sound, and the area beneath Lady N's hands suddenly feels very . . . warm.

"Ahhh . . ." the woman says. "I had a hunch there was *Vibranium* in this garish purple suit of yours."

"What?" Shuri's eyelids begin to droop.

"Shuri, FIGHT BACK!" comes a voice that isn't Riri's. Though it is familiar. The princess manages to turn her head and sees a shortish brown-skinned girl in a gray jumpsuit with her hair in braids that form a crown. She has her hands over her ears. "You've been training for this for *months*. Don't forget who you are!"

"K'Marah?" Shuri says.

The girl's eyes drop to the floor and Shuri follows them. There's a rectangular device lying facedown.

"You . . ." K'Marah falters as her French friends turn on her, back to being mindless minions. "Come ON, Shuri!"

Shuri looks at the device again. "Riri," she breathes out. "Please . . . call me."

"Riri?" Nightshade looks around at the girls in the room. "Who is Riri? Who are you talking to?" And she takes a step toward Shuri.

"Huh?" comes a voice in her ear. (Or is it in her head?)

"Call me. On the phone. Now."

"Shuri, how does—"

"Please, Riri . . ."

Shuri's eyes drift shut.

And then she's falling.

Falling . . .

Falling . . .

"WHO RUN THE WORLD? GIRLS!"

Shuri snaps back.

As it dawns on Nightshade (because that's who this woman *really* is: a villain) that something's wrong, Shuri shoves past the pain rippling down her arms (what is *on* those gloves?) and knifes her hands upward, forcing Nightshade's hands from Shuri's shoulders, and knocking the woman's head off-kilter with a blow to the chin. Nightshade reels back on now-unsteady feet.

Which the princess uses to her advantage: A quick shift in stance and a low roundhouse sweep of her right leg send the woman the rest of the way to the ground.

But Nightshade has a trick up her sleeve.

Literally.

With a flick of Nightshade's wrist—Shuri would've missed it if not for Kocha M'Shindi drilling the importance of *paying close attention*—something slides into the woman's palm, and before the princess can react, Nightshade's fingers close over it, and an earsplitting ring rips through air.

Shuri—and every girl she can see from this angle—drops to her knees with her head in her hands.

Which gives Nightshade just enough time to get to her feet.

Shuri cries out as a boot-clad foot connects with her rib cage, knocking her to her side.

Riri's voice cuts through the stabbing sensation in her eardrums: "Turn your silencer back on, Shuri!"

"I . . . can't! Hurts!"

"You have to. You're those girls' only hope!"

"I . . ."

"Come ON, Shuri! I believe in you! *Who run the world?!*"

At the sound of those four words Shuri uses all the strength she can muster to bring her hands together so she can press the button at her wrist.

The moment the noise cuts out, Shuri leaps to her feet (though her ears are still ringing). And she surges at Nightshade. Using a combo of swings, blows, and kicks that would make even M'Shindi applaud, she throws everything she's got at the Mohawked woman.

There's a chop. And a jab. And a perfectly executed butterfly kick that knocks Nightshade's noise remote thing high into the air. Shuri catches it and presses the button to shut the sound off. And the girls slowly lower their hands from their ears and rise to their feet.

When Shuri sees Nightshade crab-walking backward, she knows her job is done.

"You can signal the general now," Shuri says to Riri.

"Already on it," the girl replies.

And Shuri smiles. Because to her right, there's a group of young geniuses, some shaking their heads and some rubbing their temples, but *all* rising to their feet with their gazes set on the woman trying to get away.

And they are *not* happy.

"Girls," Shuri says, largely to herself. "Girls run the world."

21

HOMEBOUND

An unforeseen benefit to Nightshade's use of her sonic debilitation system, as Shuri calls it: The shriek displaced the auditory hypnosis sound track (also Shuri's words), and once the princess has the latter shut down, the air is eerily quiet.

After the engineering Garden girls have Nightshade restrained—using rope made of some sort of super-strong silk Nightshade herself invented ("Harsh," from Riri)—a girl named Kitty Pryde leads Shuri underground to the space *beneath* the Hive that holds the actual control room.

"By the way: What's with the bees?" the princess asks en route. "They seem an interesting thing to 'keep' in a place like this."

Kitty nods. "I remember thinking the same thing when I found out about it," she says. "I don't really *get* the whole thing because I'm tech, not entomology. But from what I was told, Lady N, like . . . *extracts*, I guess, a component of the bee venom, and uses it to make some sort of paralysis liquid?"

"Hmm . . ." Shuri wonders aloud. "I wonder if that's what was in those darts."

Kitty shrugs. "Could be."

"It would certainly make sense," Riri's voice says in Shuri's ear.

Once they reach the mainframe and Shuri is able to plant the chip, Riri is able to access the Garden's operating system. The handful of older girls round everyone up in "Hydrogen Hall," the theater-style meeting room, and while Shuri debriefs the whole lot (124 total) and assures everyone that help is on the way, Riri shuts down the perception-warping toxin pump, and makes the place visible from the outside.

Once she finishes what she hopes comes across as a pep talk, Shuri looks down at the red canvas jumpsuit she's wearing and sighs. The tech girls gave it to her and dubbed her an "honorary recruit," though the princess suspects their gift might've had something to do with the gaping holes in the shoulders of her polyethylene suit. Still though: Despite knowing this place isn't as wonderful as it seemed, part of Shuri is sad that she didn't get to spend any time here. If nothing else, she knows these girls are *her people*, and the veritable meeting of the minds was sure to have been an epic one.

She wonders what will happen to the facility once they all leave it.

Her Kimoyo card vibrates in her pocket. (Had to turn the ringer off. A near-death experience is one way to ruin an excellent song.) "Hello?"

"The fleet is arriving," Riri says.

Shuri looks around and sighs again. "Okay."

"All the doors should be wide open, elevator included. You can start sending the girls out, and they'll be sorted by region."

That gives Shuri pause. "Uhhh . . . sorted by whom?"

"Ah. Yeah, about that. I, umm . . . might've called for some backup."

"Backup?"

"Yes," Riri says without expounding. "It'll make things run a bit smoother, I think."

As the girls file out, Shuri and K'Marah find their way to each other and fall in line, side by side. They don't look at each other, and at first neither girl speaks. But as they approach the open elevator where the adventure really began, Shuri grabs K'Marah's arm to hold her back.

"It was me," she says, forcing herself to look into her friend's face. "I'm the one who said you told me about the conclave."

K'Marah tries to pull away, but Shuri holds her fast.

"I'm sorry, K'Marah. I found out about it . . . another way, and I didn't want my mother or T'Challa to know. Which doesn't make what I did excusable, but I want you to know that I told Okoye the truth. She knows it wasn't you."

K'Marah's eyes narrow and she sighs through her nose. Though she still won't look at Shuri.

The princess goes on anyway. "That letter you left . . . I read it more times than I'm willing to admit. And I've never felt so many things at once, K'Marah. Guilt over my wrongdoing. Panic that something awful was happening to you. Fear that I'd never see you again—"

"Sheesh with the gloom and doom, Shuri," K'Marah says. "I get it."

"Well, I want you to know nothing was the same without you. Not Wakanda. Not this mission. Not . . . anything."

"Shuri?"

"Yes?"

Now K'Marah turns to look Shuri in the eye. "I was gone for all of five hours."

"Not true! You were gone for *days* before that! Even if you were still *in* Wakanda—"

"Same could be said for *you*, Princess!"

"Okay, okay, fine." Shuri makes a swipe at her face. *When had she started crying?* "I just—"

But she doesn't get anything else out, because K'Marah is suddenly squeezing her so tightly, she can hardly breathe, let alone speak.

"I forgive you," the shorter (but not as shorter as she used to be) girl says. "You are pardoned. Absolved. Exonerated. In *this* court, declared not guilty."

"You are *utterly* dramatic," Shuri says, a grin tugging at the corners of her mouth. "And absolutely vital. Wakanda *needs* you, K'Marah." The princess pulls back so she can see her best friend's face. "*I* need you."

Now K'Marah swipes at *her* face. "All right, all right," she says. "Enough with the mushy-gushy. Let's get out of this place and go home."

As the girls stride into the elevator hand in hand, both startled by the sight of their shared reflection in the mirrored walls—"Whoa," K'Marah says—Shuri's mind buzzes with questions, not unlike the giant beehive. For instance: What will happen to the bees? She makes it a point to tell whoever's in charge of investigating the place that the bees are there and should be removed unharmed and delivered to a place they can thrive . . .

And then there's the question of the girls. What will happen to them when they return home? Many of them were reluctant to exit the Garden, tossing deeply forlorn looks over their shoulders on the way out, and Shuri can't say she doesn't understand why. While Shuri was only privy to a small handful of the girls' backstories, a few she's aware of involve not a small measure of poverty. Shuri wonders just how *many* of the girls were using discarded materials for their experiments. Or were on borrowed time and space in the laboratories where they were permitted to pursue their passions in their homelands.

What will happen to the likes of Pilar? Cici? Xiang? Little Syd (who was totally onto Shuri and K'Marah the first time they infiltrated)? Will all their work be for naught because they can't continue it?

Looking around the atrium space with the fake wood walls, Shuri thinks about her own wildly high-tech—and surely very expensive—laboratory back in Wakanda. And her heart clenches. What will be done with *this* place?

She sighs and resists the impulse to look back one more time as she and her very best friend in the world step through the formerly hidden entrance, and out into the bright desert day.

Where they both stop dead.

Because there in front of them is a small fleet of sleek black jets and helicopters . . . none of which are Wakandan.

"What the—" K'Marah starts and breaks off. "Is that . . . who I *think* it is?"

"Huh?"

"There, talking to Okoye."

Shuri follows K'Marah's line of sight to the general, who is standing in conversation with . . . "The red-and-gold robot?"

"Oy!" K'Marah smacks her forehead. "Do you live in a *cave*?"

Shuri is taken aback. "I mean, I don't *live* there, but I guess the space where my laboratory is located could be considered cave-like—"

"That's *Iron Man*, Shuri. One of the most famous— and richest—American Super Heroes in the biz!" K'Marah goes back to staring. "I can't even believe it."

"Well, you should," comes a deep voice from behind the girls.

They both jump and whip around. Which means

they not only see the tall, dark-brown-skinned man with the eye patch, but also what the Garden looks like from the outside when not invisible.

"Whoa," Shuri says at the same moment K'Marah says, "Aren't you *hot*?!" Because while Shuri is stunned by the matte-gunmetal, impeccably sharp-lined exterior of the two-story edifice that she knows is a giant hexagon, K'Marah is gaping at the man. Who, yes, is intensely overdressed: black dress shoes, slacks, and a turtleneck sweater . . . beneath a black trench coat.

"You're the infamous Princess Shuri of Wakanda, I take it?" the man says, locking Shuri in the gaze of his uncovered eye and crossing his arms.

"I—"

"Who wants to know?" K'Marah cuts in, stepping in front of the princess.

The man's eyebrows rise. "And who might *you* be?"

"Your worst nightmare if you don't get to talking—"

"K'Marah!"

The man chuckles and reaches into his pocket. "Colonel Nicholas Joseph Fury, Jr.," he says, flashing a shiny badge. "I'm from S.H.I.E.L.D. Which stands for the—"

"Strategic Homeland Intervention, Enforcement, and Logistics Division," Shuri says, completely in awe now.

"Ah, okay," K'Marah grumbles. "So you know the ridiculous name of some random organization from who-knows-where, but have no idea who *Iron Man* is. Typical." She shakes her head.

The man, Nick, chuckles again. "You're a spunky one," he says to K'Marah. "And yes: The princess here knows us *very* well. I understand we have *you* to thank for the mysterious cloaking technology that appeared in our design files?" He holds out a remote and points it at one of the jets. It vanishes, and the small group of adults congregated around it all stumble backward. "FURY!" one of them shouts.

"I have no idea what you're talking about," Shuri says.

"Hmm," Nick continues. "Well, whether or not *that* was you, we do have you and your Chicago-based friend Riri Williams to thank for leading us to *this* place. Tony almost didn't believe her when she reached out to him about it, but here we are."

"Tony?" Shuri says.

"STARK," from K'Marah. "Tony STARK, Shuri. As in IRON MAN!"

"Red-and-gold robot guy. Got it."

"I just wanted to personally assure you that we'll get all these young ladies back to their families safely," Nick goes on. "You have my word on that." He crosses his arms then. "Also *clearly* need to work on our cybersecurity protocols considering we've been hacked by *two* teenyboppers—"

"Who you calling a *teenybopper*?!" K'Marah barks.

It just makes Mr. Fury (what a name this guy has) laugh.

"And what will happen to this place?" Shuri says, letting her gaze drift back to the Garden building. "There's a giant beehive inside, by the way."

At first, Colonel Nicholas Joseph Fury, Jr., doesn't respond. When Shuri looks back at him, there's a smile tugging at the corner of his mouth. "We know about the bees," he says. "And don't you worry: I think S.H.I.E.L.D. can find a good use for the premises." He winks.

"Shuri! K'Marah! We need to leave, loves," Okoye shouts in their direction.

"Guess that's our cue," Shuri says with a final sigh.

"Yep!" K'Marah grabs her hand and begins to pull her in the direction of the (very much visible) *Predator*.

"Hey, Princess?" Fury says.

Shuri turns around. "Yeah?"

He rocks back on his heels and shoves his hands in his pockets. "Whereabouts are you all located? Your nation, I mean."

At this Shuri snorts. And rotates away.

"Like I'd tell you," she says without looking back.

22

EXPOSED

With one day to complete *three* assessments— including the one Shuri bombed with M'Walimu, the dinosaur tamer—the moment Okoye and the girls are back on the ground in Wakanda, Shuri goes straight to her quarters and shoves her nose into that supervillain of a Global Diplomacy textbook. She still hasn't quite figured out what she can do to help all the girls who were sent home from the Garden, but going to the conclave and seeing how this international relations stuff works feels like a decent place to start.

"You made it back from your trip," a voice says. Shuri lifts her head to find the queen mother standing in her doorway. Elegant as ever in a maroon caftan with asymmetrical "stripes" made of gold beads.

The princess sighs. Then smiles. "I did," she says.

"I trust all went smoothly?"

Shuri nods. "As silk." She nods at her mother's dress.

"Excellent. You are in the midst of your studies, I see. And I commend you. But might you permit a brief interruption?"

"Hmm?"

"I'd like to take you on a . . . field trip."

"Uhh, okay . . ." Shuri says, nervous now.

"Fret not," the queen mother continues, beckoning her daughter forward. "It won't take long."

Shuri trails the queen, her sense of dread growing with each step.

Especially when her mother leads her to the empty throne room, crosses to a back corner of it, and gently places her hand against a section of what looks like bare wall. A panel slides aside, revealing a dimly lit corridor beyond.

"Ummmm . . ."

"Come," her mother says, going through the secret doorway Shuri had no idea even existed.

The corridor dead-ends at a set of stairs that takes

the pair of Wakandan royals down a level (Shuri didn't even know there *was* another level; is this a basement?) and spits them out into a wider, brighter room where there are tables and chairs and what looks like an espresso bar at the far end. They walk through the space, passing a group of guards poring over a map, and as they're about to enter a different corridor, Ayo and Nakia come out of it.

"Princess!" Nakia says.

"Fancy meeting you here," from Ayo. With a wink.

"Take it easy on her, ey, Your Majesty?" Nakia again. She and Ayo look at each other and grin in tandem.

"Oh, hush," Shuri's mother says. "Aren't your breaks over now? Get back to your posts." And the queen mother sticks her tongue out.

(*Is this alternate reality?*)

"Come, Shuri," her mother goes on. "Almost there."

And they are. Because at the end of that passageway, the queen leads the princess into a room full of monitors, each showing a different part of the palace: There's the front drive, the loading dock, the entry hall, the kitchens, the throne room, the laundry room . . .

Her mother pulls out a chair. "Have a seat," she says.

Shuri does. Slowly.

"Center screen," her mother says. Then she gets to tapping around on what appears to be a control panel.

Shuri stares at what starts out as a view of the (empty) formal dining room with all the kingly portraits. But then it switches to a view . . . of Shuri. Inside the *Predator*, it seems, inputting coordinates. Then it switches to a view of Shuri's face looking guilty at a table as a hand—that isn't hers—swaps out two plates. K'Marah's, she realizes, during their trip to Addis Ababa with the clothier. Another cut, and Shuri sees herself cloaked in what looks like head-to-toe purple plastic, moving her hands around in the air—feeling over the then-invisible wall of the Garden. Then a cut to pieces of paper floating in midair in a six-sided office with tables all around it.

She has absolutely nothing to say.

The queen mother sets a small metal tin in front of Shuri. "Open it," she says.

Shuri clenches her jaw and does as she's told. Inside is a smattering of what look like dead ants.

Shuri's bugs.

She puts her head in her hands.

"A few weeks ago, when you told T'Challa and me that K'Marah had been the person to inform you about the maximum security conclave your brother was scheduled to attend, something felt . . . off," her mother begins. "I won't say I know the young lady as well as I know *you* do. But the notion of a Dora Milaje trainee— the *top* trainee, according to Ayo, Nakia, *and* General Okoye—sharing that information with someone very much *not* on the clearance list didn't seem plausible.

"But my beloved daughter wouldn't have *lied* to me, I thought to myself. Especially not if her aim is to *attend* this conclave she should not be aware of. So after mulling it over for a few days, I decided to take the matter to the general. She, also, was very surprised. But we had to take *your* word, Princess. *You* are first in line to the throne."

Shuri groans.

"But I was still . . . *suspicious*, I guess would be the appropriate term. In light of your previous transgressions—"

"*That* seems a bit strong, Mother."

"Don't interrupt. The point here is that Okoye and I found ourselves in the position where it was difficult to trust either of you. When *you*, of all people, approached me requesting to go on a shopping trip with the clothier, I knew you were up to something. So we had a tiny camera braided into K'Marah's hair."

"Mother!"

"Yes?" the queen says, gesturing to the tin of Shuri's eavesdropping devices.

The princess slumps down into her chair and crosses her arms. "Touché," she mutters.

"After seeing what you all got up to, I decided to have the guards sweep the palace for unauthorized surveillance devices. All these were discovered in the throne room."

What is Shuri even supposed to say?

"I trust that you don't need a lecture on the ethics of privacy invasion?"

"No," Shuri says. "Especially since I now know you were watching *me*."

"Doesn't feel very good, hmm?"

Shuri lets her head drop to the desk.

"I trust you'll find your way back to your quarters," the queen says. "T'Challa and I will see you at dinner."

She grabs the tin and turns to leave.

"Hey, Mother?" Shuri says.

"Hmm?"

"Precisely how grounded am I?"

"Oh, my sweet child," the queen says, locking eyes with the princess. "You have absolutely *no* idea."

MISSION LOG

AND HERE WE ARE: CONCLAVE DAY.

Which K'Marah and I will be spending together in my lab. While she was very much let off the hook for the lie I told, Okoye was none too thrilled with the national alarm stunt she pulled to escape the country with Lady N.

Though no one can seem to find any security footage of the culprit in action. Seems a sixty-second section of tape mysteriously vanished sometime between when I shut the thing off and when Okoye and I departed together. (Riri is enjoying the small box of gadgets she received as a token of my and K'Marah's appreciation for the missing footage.)

However, being forced to stay home today isn't all bad. K'Marah and I will be convening our first virtual C.O.W. meeting—that's Conclave of Worldrunners—with Riri, Cici, Josephine, Celeste, and Xiang Yeh. We invited our favorite Kenyan meteorological scientist, Yasha, but she's apparently still angry with me about exposing Lady N's operation.

Speaking of good ol' Tilda Johnson, her sole alias now is "Inmate 473821." She's being held indefinitely at some "supermax" facility run by S.H.I.E.L.D. hidden in a mid-American mountain range. Riri is convinced she'll have broken herself out and gotten up to some new scheme within a few months.

Anyway, on the agenda for the first virtual C.O.W.: the beginning stages of planning for a summer research camp at the Garden. Which S.H.I.E.L.D. has taken over, according to Colonel Nicholas Joseph Fury, Jr. It would be fully dual-funded by that Iron Tony Stark guy and some mysterious "grant money" Nick says S.H.I.E.L.D. received from an anonymous donor somewhere in East Africa, who apparently put "For C.O.W. Camp" in the donation memo.

("You present a compelling case for this camp, little sis," T'Challa said when I presented the proposal K'Marah and I had come up with after finding out we were both mega-grounded. "You'll make a fine world leader one day.")

Every girl who spent time at the Garden under Nightshade's thumb will receive an invitation, and we hope to bring in some of the best and brightest minds in the world to learn from and collaborate with. We've already gotten a yes from an emerging scientist (they/them pronouns) leading the research charge in the area of gender-identity formation. Nightshade was certainly off in her approach to correcting the world's ills, but she was correct about men getting more chances to change the world than anyone else, so we hope to begin leveling the playing field.

It truly will be nothing short of revolutionary.

Oh! Lastly: I passed my Global Diplomacy

retest. And have thereby completed Phase One of my Panther training.

Kocha M'Shindi has even stopped calling me "Cub."

Which leaves me with one final thought:

Who run the world?

Girls.

NIC STONE is the *New York Times* bestselling author of the novels *Dear Martin*, *Dear Justyce*, *Odd One Out*, *Fast Pitch*, and *Clean Getaway*. She was born and raised in a suburb of Atlanta, Georgia, and the only thing she loves more than an adventure is a good story about one. After graduating from Spelman College, she worked extensively in teen mentoring and lived in Israel for a few years before returning to the United States to write full-time. Having grown up with a wide range of cultures, religions, and back¬grounds, she strives to bring diverse voices and stories into her work. Learn more at nicstone.info.